EVERLY

Wilder West Book One

KAY P. DAWSON

Copyright 2021 CKN Press and Kay P. Dawson

CKN Christian Publishing
An Imprint of Wolfpack Publishing
6101 S. Fort Apache Rd, Suite 360
Las Vegas, NV 89148

ckn.christianpublishing@gmail.com

This book is a work of fiction. Any references to historical events, real people, or real places are used fictitiously. Other names, characters, places and events are products of the author's imagination, and any resemblance to actual events, places or persons, living or dead, is entirely coincidental.

eBook ISBN 978-1-64734-933-3
Paperback ISBN 978-1-64734-934-0

Everly
Print Edition
© Copyright 2021 (As Revised) Kay P. Dawson

CKN Christian Publishing
An Imprint of Wolfpack Publishing
5130 S. Fort Apache Rd. 215-380
Las Vegas, NV 89148

christiankindlenews.com

eBook ISBN: 978-1-63977-059-5
Paperback ISBN: 978-1-63977-060-1

EVERLY

CHAPTER 1

"As my final wishes in this, my last will and testament, it is put forth that in order to continue receiving money from my estate and to ensure the financial security of her mother, my eldest daughter, Everly Marie Wilder, must marry before her twenty-first birthday. If she should fail to meet this requirement, all future financial support will be cut for her mother, Caroline, and two younger sisters, Sarah Lynne and Bethany Anne Wilder."

As the words were read out loud, Everly's stomach sank. The breath flew from her lungs, as the blood drained from her face. She struggled to make a clear thought as the words echoed over and over in her head.

Looking around the room, Everly noticed the shocked looks on the faces staring back at her. She knew she'd heard the words right when she looked towards her mother. Her face had a white sheen like snow that had just hit the ground, emphasizing the blue of her eyes as she fought to hold back tears.

If not for the serious situation they were in at the

moment, the looks on her sister's faces would have made her laugh out loud. Both of them sat with mouths hung open, looking like they were ready to flee from the room out of fear for their lives.

However, laughing was the furthest thing from her mind.

"There must be some mistake. My father always knew that I had no intention of marrying, and surely would not be able to do it within the next six months. I'll be twenty-one in September, and there's no way I would even be able to find a man I could tolerate, never mind marry, in that short amount of time!"

"Everly, as your father's most trusted friend, I assure you that he was very specific in his wishes," Alistair McConnell said slowly. "He knew you never wanted to get married, and he deeply regretted that you felt that way. He also knew it was his fault that you felt you would never be able to trust a man or fall in love. This was the only way he had of ensuring that you at least tried, should something ever happen to him. I agree the timing is unfortunate, however he knew that if he wasn't here to look after his family, he had to take drastic action to ensure you'd be cared for."

The man looked around at the others uncomfortably before continuing.

"Unfortunately, with your mother's past, your father was afraid you'd all be at the mercy of anyone who wanted to take advantage of the situation. So, he thought the best way to prevent that was for you to marry someone who could take care of, and be responsible for, your family."

Mr. McConnell had been her father's lawyer, and the closest thing to a friend he had, for many years. He'd watched these girls grow from babies into the women before him. Everly knew he was a kind man, and she also knew he wasn't happy with the situation her father had kept his family in all those years. She remembered hearing them arguing about it one time when she was still young and had been playing hide and seek with her sisters. They'd never even known she was there.

Now, as she looked around his office, listening to the sounds of the carriages on the streets outside the window, she couldn't help but feel betrayed by him, too.

"I won't do it."

"He also knew you'd say that. He knew that the one thing that could convince you was your loyalty to your mother and sisters. If you don't marry as he has described in his will, all financial support will end for your mother. Your younger sisters will then be left to fend for themselves in a world that is increasingly difficult for women on their own."

"This is just like our father to be able to hurt us even after he's gone!" Beth seethed.

As the youngest, Everly knew Beth didn't have very many happy memories of her father. And seeing the pain he was causing, even in death, had raised Beth's anger. Even though their mother always tried to assure them all he cared about them in his own way, they'd never really had any reason to believe it for themselves.

"What if Everly marries someone who's a horrible man, only wanting to get his hands on our money, and who knows what else?" Beth continued. "Am I the only one who sees the possibilities of this all going wrong?"

"No. Beth, your father did think about that too." Mr. McConnell pulled at his bowtie, looking increasingly uncomfortable. He'd lowered his eyes and wasn't looking at any of them now. They knew he had more to say but was having trouble bringing himself to say it.

"There is one more condition. Before any money is to be released, it's up to me to ensure the marriage is made in love, or at least with the chance for love to happen."

Everly actually laughed out loud. There was no chance of love happening. She didn't even think such a thing existed.

She frantically looked toward her mother. Even though she could never count on her father, she always knew her mother would be able to fix anything. It had always been that way when she was growing up.

"There must be a way around this," Caroline stated, showing a calmness that no one in the room felt. "And if there isn't, we'll figure something out. I can't believe, after everything, Thomas would leave me and his daughters destitute."

Everly's father had been in and out of their lives and had never been able to give them any stability. She was angry at the fact he'd never made them a legitimate family. They didn't even have his last name.

But nothing could have prepared her for this final act of treachery.

"I assure you, leaving you destitute is the last thing he would have ever wanted," Mr. McConnell said. "But he also worried that his daughters would be left without a man to provide them with not only financial security, but to offer them protection from the evils in the world. You can have no doubts that Thomas cared about you all in his own way, and he felt tremendous guilt for the unfairness of how you were forced to live over these past years.

"So, before he left to board that ship to England, he made sure everything was in order should he not return. His concerns were for his daughters, and for you as well, Caroline, above all else. He wasn't a perfect man, and he felt such regret for not being able to be more to his daughters."

If Everly had any lingering doubts about how much she hated her father, this final act erased them. Even from beyond the grave, her father was determined to destroy her happiness, as he'd done to her mother for so many years.

❧

"EVERLY, you need to just sit down so we can discuss this like adults!"

"Ma, don't you get it? He never cared about any of us! He never gave you, or us for that matter, the love, or the life we all deserved!" Everly stomped around the room, with her hands clenched in fists at her sides. "How is it fair that even when he's dead he's still able to control our lives? I will not do it. I'll find a way to look after this family without his money."

"It's not just about you, Everly!" her younger sister, Sarah, cried. "You need to think of us, too! If you don't at least consider doing what he's asked, what will happen to the rest of us? What about our futures? I'd like to have the opportunity to find a man to love, and who'll love me in return, but that isn't likely to happen if I have to work as a whore in order to stay alive!"

"Sarah!" Everly and Beth both shouted at her as the words echoed in the air, hanging like a fog that would never lift. As the words left her mouth, Sarah looked at her mother, noticing the tight lines that creased her tired face.

"I'm sorry, Mama. I didn't mean it." Sarah went over and knelt before her mother, taking her hands in her own.

A silence enveloped the room that no one seemed willing to break.

"My past is no secret to you girls, as much as I wish it were," Caroline finally said.

Everly watched her reach out and gently brush away the tear that was rolling down her daughter's cheek.

"You all need to remember something. No matter how angry you are with your father for not giving you the life you dreamed of you should also remember that if not for him, I would've spent my life living the existence that you so dread – an existence I would never wish on anyone, especially my daughters. And neither could he. He knew with your anger toward him, and your distrust of men because of our situation, it was likely none of you would ever consider finding a man to love and care for you."

Caroline stood up, helping Sarah to stand. She walked over and looked out the window, rubbing her hands together as Everly imagined she was trying to erase the memories that were pushing themselves into her mind.

"He couldn't bear the thought of any of you ending up on the streets, or having to resort to anything horrible to survive, like I did. He may not have been a perfect father, but he did care in his own way, about all of you. He was forced to marry out of duty to his family's name. Marrying me was never going to be an option for him. He loved me, though, and he loved all of you too. He just never learned how to handle the circumstance he'd been put in.

"In a perfect world, women wouldn't need a man to protect her and offer her a better future, but sadly we have to admit this is what we are up against.

"We could survive on our own, and we might have a good life. But the obstacles we would face are more than you can even imagine. As much as it angers us, and seems unfair, we can't deny we are still living in a man's world. The sad fact remains that women are often at the mercy of the men around us."

Caroline turned back around. There were tears in her eyes, and she seemed to have aged years in the past few days. Tufts of hair had come loose from her bun, and dark circles under her eyes betrayed the lack of sleep she'd been suffering from since learning of Thomas' death. She looked towards her oldest daughter.

"So, Everly, while having to marry a man who can offer you that kind of security, and possibly even a chance at love, might not be the future you'd planned for yourself, I hope that you will at least consider it. Remember, the results of your decision won't only affect you."

With those words, Caroline walked out the door, carrying her head high with a grace that, had they not known the truth about who she was, would've made even the highest ladies in society bow down as she walked by.

Everly looked after her mother, then back to her sisters, who both sat looking at their hands crossed in their laps. She quietly sat down in the closest chair.

The weight of the responsibility for the future of her family seemed to push her down even further into the chair. Her skirts felt like lead, and she was afraid to speak for fear she would break down and cry in front of her sisters.

"What will we do, Everly?" Beth quietly asked, looking at Everly with worry in her eyes. Even though she was only seventeen, she was already well known as a spitfire. Without a male figure to discipline and keep her in line, Beth had been allowed more freedom than many others her age. She spent a great deal of time helping out down at the stables, and had no trouble riding bareback.

Hearing the words spoken so softly from the one person Everly was sure would be angrier than her, and who she'd never seen afraid, tore at her heart. As the oldest daughter, she'd always done her best to protect her sisters and make sure they were looked after.

Now she desperately wanted someone to tell her what to do.

The realization that she was now entirely responsible for the future of her family felt like a pair of hands grabbing her around her neck and choking her. She couldn't help but see the face behind those hands as the one of her own father.

8

CHAPTER 2

As Ben walked in from the pasture, he could see a carriage pulled up by the house. His oldest niece Olivia came running toward him as he neared the barn.

"Uncle Ben! That horrible lady from the store in town is here and she says she wants to talk to you!"

He inwardly cringed, even while he thought he should correct her manners. "That isn't nice to call her names, Olivia – even if she is horrible." He winked.

"Tell her I'll be right there once I get Bandit settled back in the barn."

He watched Olivia run back to the house, and as he led his horse into the barn, he ran all the possible reasons through his mind of what Hazel Hayes, the town's meddling store owner, would want with him. No matter what, he knew in his gut it wasn't going to be good. It never was with her.

To make matters worse, he'd almost married her daughter before calling off the engagement. Hazel Hayes had wanted her daughter Margaret married to him at all costs. There weren't many options around High Ridge, and Ben knew that he was prime husband material for a woman who wanted her daughter married to someone who had money to bring into the marriage.

In all fairness, he had cared for Margaret at one time, and would've married her had he not found out her true nature.

When his cousin Jake, whom he trusted with his life, had told him that he'd found Margaret kissing the blacksmith from town, he'd promptly called the wedding off. In order to preserve her dignity after Margaret begged him not to tell anyone the truth, he'd never told anyone the reasons other than he wasn't ready for marriage.

Hazel had taken the news hard. Ben knew that Margaret had never loved him, and he sensed she'd been almost relieved when he called off the engagement. The fact that there weren't many available women for marriage had been one of the reasons he'd allowed himself to be pushed towards Margaret by her mother in the first place.

Hazel had complete control in her family and had decided for Margaret that she should welcome a courtship from Ben. The feelings she had for the blacksmith hadn't mattered to her mother. She'd been told it was just an infatuation and that a union with Ben Montgomery would give her a much better life. She'd have the money and the name of an influential family in town, and that was all that mattered to Hazel Hayes.

And now, as Ben walked toward the house, he knew that the woman standing on his front porch wasn't coming for a pleasant neighborly visit.

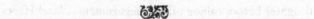

"BEN, how nice of you to finally come to the house!" Hazel welcomed him sourly.

"I have cattle to care for, and after a morning ride checking on the cattle and my land, my horse needed to be put away properly. I assure you I came as quick as I could." He tried to keep his tone as civil as was possible through clenched teeth.

"To what do I owe this visit, Hazel?"

Hazel looked around at the people standing on the porch. The two little girls who'd been left in Ben's care after their parents were killed in a carriage accident looked at Ben with concern in their eyes. Mary O'Hara, the older lady who came to care for the kids and clean the house during the day, also stood on the porch, watching the exchange. She must've sensed that the kids might not want to hear what was about to be said, because she corralled the girls together and took them back into the house for breakfast.

Hazel watched them go and then turned back toward Ben.

"I'm sure you're aware, that a single man living out here with no one else to care for those girls is considered highly inappropriate."

"Considered by whom?" he countered. "By you?"

Hazel didn't even miss a breath. "Well, not just me. There are other ladies in town who I've been speaking to, and we all feel that the girls need a mother figure. A woman who can raise them and offer them the guidance only a woman can. Living out here with just you and the men who work around your ranch, is not acceptable."

"And I suppose you've made sure all of these other ladies know exactly how inappropriate it is? And the group of you have decided that you know better what is best for my nieces? Is that right?"

He walked toward Hazel with a look in his eyes that would've told anyone else that they were treading on thin ice. But she didn't seem to notice.

"It doesn't matter how it came up. What matters is that we are only thinking of the best interests of the girls. Without a woman to guide them and preserve their dignity out here, we need to consider other options." She tried to stand a bit taller as he kept walking dangerously close to her.

"Are you really thinking of the best interests of my nieces, or more about the best interests of your daughter? Do you feel that by threatening me with the possible loss of these girls you can force me into marrying her?" Ben asked with a quiet calmness that was not reflected by the anger in his eyes.

"Oh! I'm shocked that you would think such a thing, Ben Montgomery! That's not the reason for my concern at all. However, now that you bring it up, marrying Margaret would solve your problem." Hazel pushed, obviously still not aware of how dangerously close Ben was to losing his temper completely.

"Let me tell you one thing, and I want you to remember these words as you get in your carriage and head back to town. My nieces are my family. They are mine. They will be cared for living here with me, someone who loves them, far better than they could ever be cared for anywhere else. Nothing you say, or you and your meddling friends from town do, will ever change that." With that, he put his face directly in front of hers to make sure she heard every word.

"If you do anything to try and have them taken away from me, you'll regret ever hearing my name. Do I make myself clear?" He kept his eyes on hers while he spoke the words.

"Very clear." Finally realizing she should've kept a safer distance, Hazel swallowed hard while taking a step back.

"But I assure you before I leave, I'll do everything in my power to have those girls moved somewhere that'll provide them with the upbringing only a woman can give. And if you can't figure out a way to give that to them here, then they'll be taken somewhere they can."

With that, Hazel climbed into her carriage and rode away, leaving a cloud of dust in the air that whirled around as fast as the thoughts in his head. It took every bit of control he had to not grab the reins of her horse as she went by him, and tell her exactly what he thought of her at that moment. He was sure, though, that he wouldn't be able to control his temper, and he might say something he would only regret.

THAT EVENING, as Ben sat on the porch with Jake, he filled him in on everything Hazel said. The words had played on his mind all day, and while he meant what he'd said to her about taking the kids from him, doubt still crept in, stealing away the certainty that he'd be able to win this battle.

Hazel had many people in the community bowing down to her. Her overbearing demeanor scared most citizens from ever speaking their minds to her about how they really felt. She was able to control the thoughts and actions of the entire congregation in their small church simply by stating her opinions. The flock followed her as though no one else could have any ideas of their own.

That is what worried Ben the most. If it were anyone other than Hazel Hayes, he would have no doubt he'd be able to win when going head-to-head with them. But she had connections, and she had a way of convincing entire communities to follow her lead.

"Well, she won't win, Ben. We won't let her," Jake assured him.

"I wish I could be that certain, Jake. If you'd seen the look on her face; she isn't going to back down easily." Ben leaned forward in his chair and ran his hands through his hair.

"You know you can always tell her what really happened with Margaret. You can threaten to let the community know that you took the blame for breaking off the engagement only to protect Margaret's reputation. She won't want her daughter's name being dragged through the mud, so surely she'd back off then."

Jake was still angry about how Hazel had tried to manipulate the whole courtship between his cousin and her daughter. He'd never wanted Ben to be dragged into that family and was secretly relieved the day he'd walked behind the blacksmith shop and found Margaret in the blacksmith's arms.

She'd begged him not to tell Ben. She was terrified of what her mother would say. Andy, the blacksmith, was young and didn't have the money and prestige that Hazel felt Margaret would get by marrying Ben. He'd stood there looking helpless and scared, knowing full well that his future in High Ridge could be at risk if Hazel found out.

Jake had told Ben only to save him from the fate of being humiliated by marrying someone who would never love him. Not to mention sparing him from having to spend the rest of his life related to a woman as vile as Hazel.

"I won't stoop to her level, Jake. I can't do that. Even

though I never loved her, Margaret is still a friend and I wouldn't want to hurt her. She can't help who she's in love with any more than she can help her mother being a meddling old bat who has nothing better to do than control everyone around her."

"Even if it means losing the two most important people in your life?" Jake quietly asked.

Ben looked out across the pasture that spread as far as his eyes could see in the growing darkness of the evening. The colors of the sun going down over the hill reflected on the green grass like a kaleidoscope he'd seen at a fair when he was just a child.

"There has to be another way. I'll do everything in my power to keep those girls with me. My sister meant everything to me, and I always looked out for her. I couldn't save her from dying, but I will not let her down now. Those girls will be staying with me, even if I have to marry the next woman who walks into town. Somehow, I'll find a way to give Hazel that mother figure she feels they so desperately need, without marrying her daughter."

They sat in silence, listening to the crickets and other sounds of the night starting to come to life. In the distance, an owl could be heard awakening.

Jake broke the silence. "Well, what if you found a woman who didn't live here, and convinced her to move here to marry you? Would you consider it?"

Ben looked at his cousin like he'd lost his mind.

"When do I have time to go out and find a woman, never mind take the time needed to court her and make her fall in love with me? I don't even have the time between my ranch and caring for the kids on my own to go into High Ridge for an evening, never mind having to go somewhere else!"

"Well, I have an idea – but you have to promise to hear me out." Jake held his hands up as he tried to hurry and share his idea with Ben before he changed his mind.

"Today when I was in town, I went in to pick up some supplies, and I overheard a couple of men talking about putting an ad in a magazine looking for a bride from back east."

Ben was already interrupting, "I'm not putting an order in for a woman to come out here to marry me the way I would buy cattle! I could end up with a woman worse than Hazel Hayes, and then I'd be stuck with her!"

"I said to hear me out!" Jake interrupted. "Just listen. Apparently, you write to the woman first a few times and you both get to decide if you think you're a match. You don't need to end up with just anyone – you can pick one after writing a bit. When you both agree she should come west, you send her the money for a ticket and make arrangements for her to come out. It's that simple." Jake tried to make it sound better than it was, even though he was just as skeptical as Ben.

"How can you feel a connection with someone without seeing them first? And who's to say she wouldn't be filling my head with lies just to get my money for a ticket?" Ben stood up and leaned against the post to the stairs leading down from the porch. He took a sip of his tea while he thought about what Jake had said.

"And besides, what kind of woman needs to answer ads from complete strangers? There would have to be something wrong with her that she wasn't able to find a suitable husband back east."

"Ben, hundreds of women are coming west to get married. There can't be something wrong with all of them. Maybe their choices aren't so good where they live, just like us out here. Maybe they want an adventure, and love, and to make a better life for themselves. That doesn't mean there's anything wrong with them."

"You sound like you know a lot about this. Hiding something from me, Jake?" Ben grinned as he pushed forward from the post and sat back down in his chair. He'd been restless since his encounter with Hazel this morning.

Even with the increasing dark of the night, he could see Jake look sheepishly at his boots. "Well, I admit I was curious, so I went over and asked the men what they were talking about. Apparently, you make an ad telling about yourself, and the ad will be put in magazines back east. You don't even have to answer any of the letters you receive, and you don't have to send for a woman unless you're certain."

Ben looked at Jake and shook his head. He was sure he must have been knocked off his horse and hit his head.

Jake wasn't giving up, though. "What have you got to lose by trying, Ben? If that old busybody Hazel wants to back you into a corner, maybe this is a way you can push back. If you can find another woman to look after the kids, without needing to resort to marrying Margaret, wouldn't it be a great feeling to rub that in her face?"

Jake always told it like it was, Ben thought. And he was right. He had nothing to lose by writing to someone, and everything to lose if he couldn't find a wife. He'd told Hazel he would do anything to keep them with him, he just hadn't thought that would include putting himself on the market like one of his bulls.

CHAPTER 3

"Have you thought about what you're going to do, Everly?" Sarah asked.

Sarah was only a year and a half younger, and along with Beth, was Everly's closest friend.

"I still don't want to talk about it, Sarah. You know how I feel about getting married and being forced to do it makes me so angry. Our father never cared about anyone but himself, and now I'm paying for his mistakes. Even from the grave he wants to have control."

"I know it isn't fair, and if I could, I'd change places with you in an instant," Sarah said. "I think the chance of finding someone to fall in love with and marry sounds so exciting!" Sarah smiled and rested her chin in her hands. She was always reading books that talked about true love and thought the idea of falling in love was wonderful. Her sisters just rolled their eyes whenever she started to talk about it.

"Falling in love is just something that happens in one of your books," Everly said. "It doesn't happen in real life, and the sooner you realize that, the easier it will be for you when you get older. I'll do what I have to do to keep you all safe and secure but falling in love won't be one of those things." Everly pushed her chair back from the table and walked over to the stove where the kettle was starting to boil.

"If I do decide to marry, it will strictly be on my own terms. I won't let any man take control of my heart, only to destroy it when it suits him." She had her own ideas of love, and they didn't match those of her sister's.

"Everly, you know Pa loved Mama. He may not have been able to be her husband, and we all know he was no saint, but surely you don't doubt how he felt about her, and us!" Sarah had always been such an innocent when it came to the relationship her parents had. She was someone who always saw only the good in people, whereas Everly and Beth had seen worse.

Everly turned back toward her sister at the table and smiled. "You always believe the best in people, Sarah; that's what I love about you. But I'm older, and I saw how Mama would cry when he left, not knowing when he'd be back. I saw her beg him to stay with us, to let us be a real family, and I know how it tore at her heart to be in love with a man who could never give her the life she'd dreamed about."

Sarah wasn't backing down. "No, she didn't have the life she dreamed of, but she also had a better life than she would have if not for Pa. Remember that. When her parents died and left her alone on the streets, she was left to take care of herself. I would never judge her for what she had to do. When our father came along and took her away from a life that would've surely killed her, he gave her a second chance."

Sarah came to Everly's side at the stove, reaching for the teacups from the shelf.

"You have to stop being so angry at the past and look toward the future. I'm sure both of them wish they'd done things differently, but that can't be changed now. Now we need to figure out how we can make sure Mama is taken care of, and that we can have a chance at a better life too."

"When did you get so insightful?" Everly teased her sister, taking the kettle from the stove and pouring water into the teapot.

"Well, I have a pretty good role model to look up to who's taught me well," Sarah pointed out. "I know this is going to be hard for you, but I know you'll find a way to work it all out. You always do."

Hearing those words, Everly knew she had to do whatever she could to ensure that her sister's faith in her was justified. She just wished she knew what the answer was this time, because she'd run through every possibility in her mind a hundred times and wasn't any closer to figuring it out.

❧

"Look at this, Everly! Have you ever seen anything like it?"

Everly glanced at what Sarah was holding in her hands. She and her sisters had stopped at the mercantile just a few blocks away from their small upstairs apartment above the hotel where their mother worked as a cook and cleaner.

"What is it?" Everly was busy going over their list with the shopkeeper and wasn't paying much attention to what Sarah was looking at so intently. Beth was over looking at a saddle showcased at the front of the store.

"It looks like some kind of magazine that advertises

men looking for women to marry! This has to be a sign, Everly!" Sarah was so excited and hadn't noticed that others were starting to stare. One woman stood at the back of the shop keeping her back to the girls. She'd been in the shop when they entered, but they hadn't noticed her.

Everly tried not to roll her eyes as she took the magazine from Sarah's hands to see for herself. Opening to the first page of "Matrimony West", she saw ad after ad from men who were searching for a bride.

"Surely this isn't a real thing, is it?" Sarah asked Everly as she crowded in, getting up on her toes to peer over Everly's shoulder at the magazine that'd been ripped from her hands. Beth had walked over as she heard the commotion.

"I've heard of it," Everly replied while turning the pages.

"Heard of what?" Beth was now trying to look over Everly's other shoulder to see what they were looking at.

"It's nothing! Just a magazine that caters to desperate people who can't find someone to marry them on their own." Everly closed the pages and set it back on the counter.

"I honestly didn't believe this was really something people would do. What kind of woman would head out west to marry a complete stranger, someone who might turn out to be a horrible person?"

"A woman who was running out of time, and needed to find someone to marry her so that her family would be looked after?" Sarah tried to sound innocent, but they all knew she meant it.

Beth hit her shoulder with the back of her hand. "Sarah! Everly doesn't need to stoop to answering some ad for a husband! She'll fix this without the help of any man. She always does."

Everly shot Sarah a look that made the younger woman avert her eyes. She hated knowing that all of this rested on her shoulders, and she felt the pressure even more when her youngest sister showed such faith in her being able to fix it.

"Well, it doesn't matter anyway. I'd never hop on a train to go thousands of miles to marry someone who might not even be who he says he is. Help me get our things and let's head back home." Everly started gathering the few items they'd been sent to pick up.

Walking away with her hands full, Everly never noticed Sarah put the money down to pay for the magazine, and quietly fold it up into her bag. Beth did, but was silenced by the look Sarah shot her direction as they followed Everly from the store.

The lady at the back of the store slowly turned and headed toward the counter where the magazine was displayed. She picked up her own copy, paid and followed the girls from the store.

CHAPTER 4

The sun shone its last rays through the window, casting shadows on the table where Everly sat patching up holes in clothing sent up earlier by the hotel guests. She always helped her mother as much as she could with the work, and sewing was something she found helped her to relax.

While she moved the needle and thread through the fabric, she thought back to her conversation with her sisters that afternoon. She knew Sarah wanted to believe in love and dreamed of finding someone who'd show her what real love was, but Everly worried that she was only setting herself up for disappointment. Beth was more like her, and likely would never find anyone she could trust enough to marry.

She worried so much about Sarah. She was going to have to watch out for her so she wouldn't get used by any man trying to use her kindness to his advantage. Beth was a different story. In fact, Everly worried more about any man who might think he could handle a girl like

Beth, who didn't believe she needed a man to ever take care of her!

Pricking her finger with the needle, Everly stuck it in her mouth to stop the bleeding. She couldn't stop the thoughts in her head which were distracting her, so she set her sewing down and walked over to look out the window at the people bustling around on the street below.

She knew deep down that her father had cared for her mother, but she also knew that he'd made the decision to be married to another woman. She couldn't understand how he could have done that.

He'd never stood up to his own parents who'd forced him to marry someone he didn't love, and that was what made all of this sting that much more. The fact that he was now doing the very same thing to her, by forcing her to marry before she could have a chance to find love on her own, was so unfair.

The setting sun moved and caused a glare out of the corner of her eye. She turned and saw something sitting on the edge of the chair in the corner. Wondering what it could be, she walked over, and saw the magazine from the store this afternoon. Sarah must have picked it up anyway.

Looking at the magazine, her curiosity won out and she sat down to leaf through the pages.

Staring back at her was ad after ad from men offering better lives to any women willing to take a risk and head west. Some of them were sad, some seemed too good to be true. Those were the ones that made her roll her eyes as she read, knowing that it was very likely most of these men were not telling the complete truth. Some naive woman would likely end up heading out for a better life, and end up with nothing like what was being promised.

"Wanted: A woman who is honest, intelligent, who is willing to make a home with a man possessed of some means."

"An intelligent gentleman of 26 years of age, 5 feet 2 inches, would like to correspond with a woman with a loving disposition, not sour, who desires adventure and a chance to provide many healthy children to the union."

Did women actually fall for these ads? How could they ever know what they were really heading into by agreeing to marry these men? Some of them sounded downright strange.

"Everly? What are you reading?" Beth startled Everly as she walked into the room, causing her to drop the magazine on the floor.

Beth bent down to pick it up. Beth's eyebrows were raised, and it was easy to see she wasn't impressed with what she saw.

"Why do you have this here? You can't seriously be thinking about doing this!"

"Sarah must have picked it up today when we were leaving the store. Obviously, she didn't believe me when I said I wouldn't be interested in something like this."

As though she knew they were talking about her, Sarah walked into the room.

"What?" She looked innocent as she looked back and forth between her sisters. She smiled then as she saw the magazine Beth was holding in her hands.

"Oh, you found it! Did you look at it?" Sarah walked over, took the magazine from Beth and opened it up.

"Sarah, I just don't think answering an ad for a bride to move out west is a good idea. How would I know that I wasn't ending up with someone who drinks and who beats women? The ads in those kind of magazines are for desperate men, and they can't be trusted." Everly felt like she was wasting her breath on Sarah, as she watched her turn the pages and smile at some of the ads she was reading.

Beth walked over and ripped the magazine out of Sarah's grip, waving it at her as she spoke. "She's right, Sarah. Men can't be trusted when they are right in front of us, never mind when they are placing an ad for some poor woman to put her faith in him, expect him to be a good man when she has never even met him, and then head thousands of miles from home to spend her life with him!"

"You're both so ornery. These men have few women out west to choose from, that is the only reason they have to place ads for those of us back east. It has nothing to do with them being horrible men. Some of them likely are, but not all of them can be bad!" She glared at Beth, then grabbed the magazine back as she went and sat down in the chair by the window. Everly was sure that the magazine would be ripped to pieces by the end of the evening.

Sarah continued while she looked down at the magazine. "Why can't you just give it a chance? You have nothing to lose by writing to one or two men who might appeal to you! You don't have to go out there unless you feel you can trust him after writing to him a few times. There is nothing saying you have to marry a man just because you wrote him a letter!

"What other options do we have, Everly? You're running out of time, and if you don't find someone soon, we'll be left destitute, and what will happen to us then?" Everly knew Sarah was right, but she still wasn't sure marrying some strange man was the answer she was looking for.

Everly sat down, resting her head in her hands. Why did this all have to be so complicated? Just a few short days ago their lives seemed so boring and ordinary. Now she felt like her life had been taken out of her hands, and nothing seemed to be happening the way she wanted.

Sarah had to know how much this was distressing her, because she reached out and put her hand on top of Everly's, then softened her voice as she continued. "You know there aren't any men around here that you are interested in. And, even if there were, too many of them know Mama's history, and won't offer us a true marriage. You know what happened with Floyd. He courted you, but then made it clear he'd never be able to marry you. His family name wouldn't allow it. Is that what you want for yourself, too? You hated the life Mama had with our father."

Everly cringed as she remembered that whole fiasco with Floyd. She'd thought he might love her, but soon saw what he truly saw her as just because of her mother's past.

"Here we can't get away from who we are. The west has men who are willing to give us a chance without caring about our pasts. I don't judge Mama for anything she's done, but the sad truth is, everyone else around here does."

The sisters sat there in silence as they let the truth of those words sink in. Sarah was right. Everly was running out of time, and if she were going to marry, it wouldn't be to a man who believed that because of her parent's past, she'd never be good enough to offer her more.

Beth looked at her with a sad expression, crossing her arms in front of her. "Whatever you decide to do, Everly, I'll support you. No man will hurt you, that's a promise."

Everly smiled at her, knowing in her heart that Beth would be apt to kill any man who did hurt her, and she felt comfort knowing her sisters were always going to be there for her. They'd help her get through all of this.

Everly looked back down at the magazine Sarah was holding out to her, and taking it in her own hands, she opened to the first page. She knew she had to at least try something. Her family depended on her.

"Here, Everly, let's look together." Sarah pulled her chair over next to her.

"Ya, who knows, it might even be fun!" Everly shot her head up to look at Beth with a raised eyebrow as she heard those words. "What? You never know!" Beth defended herself, even though she knew neither of her sister's really believed she felt that way. She pulled another chair to the other side of Everly.

Looking at both of her sister's heads bowed looking at the magazine, Everly felt her heart fill with love. The three of them had always stuck together and she wouldn't trade a moment of her life with them for anything in the world. She also knew she'd be willing to do whatever she had to do to make sure they were taken care of.

❦

After what seemed like hours of reading endless ads from men seeking "woman of means", "woman with good childbearing years left", and "woman who can cook", the girls felt like there truly might not be any men out there offering Everly anything more than a life as a housekeeper. Even though she was being forced to marry, they hoped she could still have the chance to find love as well.

"Look at this one!" Sarah poked the ad so hard Everly

lost her grip on the pages. She grabbed the magazine from Everly's hands before she could stop her.

Sarah stood up and walked around the room while she read out loud. "Gentleman of 26 years, hardworking and kind. Seeking a woman to help him raise two young nieces left in his care in exchange for a good home, a family and the promise to be treated fairly and honorably. Will only reply to women who can promise to care for the girls like they are their own, and who is prepared to be honest in their replies."

"He seems more interested in finding someone to care for the kids than he is in finding a wife." Sarah walked back over to Everly and handed her back the magazine as she sat down.

"He's likely 5 feet tall, bald and wheezes when he breathes," Beth muttered under her breath.

Everly and Sarah both shot her a glare, then as the three of them were looking at each other, the pressure of the past few days and the situation they were in finally got the best of them. As they sat there laughing out loud, their mother ran into the room hearing all the noise.

"What's wrong? Are you girls all right?"

"Fine, Mama. We were just fantasizing about the perfect man Everly will be marrying!" Beth managed to get out between giggles.

Everly smiled, looking down to reread the ad. Something seemed different about this one, and she couldn't quite put her finger on it. Maybe it was the way he didn't make any false promises, and that he mentioned how important honesty was to him. That was something Everly could relate to, even if she knew deep down she couldn't tell him everything about her mother's past.

Seeing him show more concern about the children left in his care than gaining anything for himself, tugged at her heart strings. She knew how it felt to have the responsibility of caring for loved ones, and the lengths you'd be willing to go for their happiness.

Like Sarah said, what did she have to lose?

With that, she took out a piece of paper and started to think of what she should say in her letter to him.

CHAPTER 5

"**M**ister Jake dropped off some more mail for ye on his way back from town," Mary told him as he walked in the door.

As Ben took his hat off to hang on the hook, Olivia and her younger sister Elizabeth ran to him with arms outstretched. He picked them both up easily and swung them in circles before kissing the tops of their heads and setting them back down.

He looked over to where his housekeeper held out the pile of mail to him.

"Are there more letters from ladies wanting to marry you, Uncle Ben?" Elizabeth asked excitedly.

The girls had overheard Ben and Jake talking about writing an ad for a wife, and they'd been overflowing with excitement ever since. Every time a letter came from another woman back east, they insisted on reading the letter to see if it was a lady suitable for their Uncle Ben. So far, there hadn't been any women he had any interest in responding to. Just because he was marrying out of a duty to keep the girls with him, he also would not compromise on the kind of woman he insisted he have to help him raise them.

Ben took the letters and looked through them. There were three letters this time, and he was almost too exhausted to even be bothered looking at them, but the look on the girls' faces indicated that they were not going to leave him alone until he did.

It had only been a year since their parents had been in a carriage accident, leaving them to grow up with Ben. He was the only living relative, besides his father who also lived in a small house on the property. He'd always looked after his sister while they were growing up, as the older brother who always had her tagging along behind him. He'd been devastated when she was killed, and he had vowed that he'd do his best to raise her girls the best he could.

They missed their parents terribly, and he knew that the possibility of having a woman they could look on as a mother was something they both longed for.

He sat down on his chair and both girls crawled up on either side of him while he read the letters.

The first one was from a woman in New York, and as he read about her many outstanding qualities, he couldn't help but wonder how she could be so wealthy and beautiful and yet still be single. Doubting the sincerity of that letter, he opened the second one. The smell of perfume almost choked him as he immediately recognized the desperation of a woman who obviously thought the flowery smell would help him look past the fact that she was 10 years his senior and had six children of her own.

Every letter had been the same. Flowery promises of beauty and intelligence, ability to cook and clean, wealth, some even going as far as to professing love for him if he would send for them. No personality to any of the women writing, and none of them seemed to understand the most important reason he had placed the ad in the first place.

He genuinely felt bad for these women who were obviously so desperate for a chance at a new life, some likely running out of options. He couldn't get past the fact that none of them seemed to be the right one to care for the girls. There just wasn't any woman who'd stood out from the others.

Maybe he was asking for too much.

He sighed as he opened the last letter from Chicago. He braced himself to read more empty words.

"Dear Mr. Montgomery,

"I read your ad with interest, as I noted that your concern lies more in finding someone to help you raise your nieces, than in finding a companion for yourself. The idea of having a secure home and a family is very appealing to me, but before I continue, in all fairness I feel I need to be honest with you.

"Marriage is not something I had ever really wanted for myself; however, I have been placed in a situation that requires me to marry before my twenty-first birthday in less than six months' time. I've been raised in a family with a mother and two younger sisters who I have helped to look after since we were all young.

"Under these circumstances, I am forced to take matters into my own hands and find a husband who I can trust. I have read many ads that seemed lacking in sincerity, but I found your ad different. You seem honorable, which is why I have responded to you. I hope that this is the case, and that my trust has not been placed in the wrong hands.

"I can offer you friendship, but that is all I can promise you at this time. Perhaps it can lead to more in the future, while I help you in the raising of your wonderful nieces. I would be

lying if I said I could give you more than that without knowing you first.

"In return, I would ask for your honesty in all matters, so that we could hopefully grow to trust and care for each other in time.

"I hope you will consider a correspondence to see if we would be a suitable match. I look forward to hearing from you.

"Sincerely,

"Everly Wilder"

Ben had to read through the letter another time to be sure he'd read it correctly. Surely this wasn't a real letter written by a real woman!

She sounded like she'd rather die alone as a spinster than to ever have to marry, and yet she was being forced for some reason to respond to an ad from a stranger with the possibility of marrying. She was offering him nothing more than what she honestly felt was possible without meeting him. There were no false promises of love and devotion, just raw and complete honesty and what she wanted from him.

He almost had to laugh at the seriousness of her words. For someone who was obviously in need of a husband, she sure didn't seem willing to go out of her way to make him fall head over heels for her.

It was almost as though she was hoping he wouldn't reply. He knew for that reason alone, he had to send a letter back to her.

He looked at each of the girls who couldn't read yet, but they sensed that this one was different by the look on his face. He was smiling and looked like he was about to play a huge trick on someone.

"I think I need to find me some paper. And if you girls have any idea of what I should say to a woman who I could end up marrying, I could use your help in writing this letter!"

Both girls leapt from his lap and ran off to get him everything he'd need to write the letter. Mary looked over at Ben, where he still sat in the chair, reading the letter one more time.

In all the months she'd been helping him, she had only seen him smile like that at his nieces. The hardness of his face was softened as he smiled at the words on the paper.

She knew he was taking a huge risk, and she desperately hoped it would all work out.

CHAPTER 6

"**O**h my goodness, Everly – he wrote back!"
Sarah gushed as she ran through the door
almost knocking her over.

Without wanting to seem too anxious, Everly took
the letter from her sister's hands. She'd tried not to think
too much over the past few weeks about the man she'd
written to, but there was something that kept pulling her
thoughts to him. What did he look like? What kind of
man was he? All questions she thought she didn't really
care about yet kept niggling at her thoughts.

She sat down and opened the letter, turning her
shoulder to Sarah who was trying to read it from
behind her.

"Dear Miss Wilder,

*"Thank you for your letter. I must confess that yours is the
only one I've been able to bring myself to respond to. Your
honesty is refreshing, and I will admit my curiosity has got the
better of me in regards to your situation.*

"I assure you that I am trustworthy, and although you did not ask, my nieces assure me that I am handsome enough.

"As you said, finding a woman who is capable of helping me raise the girls is my top priority, however finding a companion who I could spend time with and possibly enjoy a happy future together is not something I would be against either.

"I own a ranch of about 500 acres, with cattle and some farmland. My father lives in a small house on the property and looks after breeding our horses, which we also sell. The town we live near, High Ridge, Wyoming, is small; only about 300 people. But there is everything a person would need, so I would hope that coming from living in a city to a small town out west wouldn't be too much of a stretch for a woman.

"My nieces are Olivia, who is 7 and Elizabeth who is 5 years old. Their parents were killed in a carriage accident, and my father and I are their only living relatives. I'm doing my best to raise them as my sister would have wanted me to, but I fear that they do need a woman's influence to help them as they grow.

"I'm a hard worker, but I also try to make time to spend with the girls. It's difficult though, to balance my time. I have a woman who comes out from town during the day to help and to look after the house duties. Her name is Mary O'Hara, and she's been a tremendous help to me since the girls have come here to live.

"I would like to know more about you, if you would be inclined to share more with me. As you may have already gathered, I was reluctant to place an ad for a wife in the first place. However, I do understand the need for a woman to help raise the girls, and there are not many out west to choose from. I want someone who will be a good influence, who will hopefully come to love the girls, and maybe even me, one day.

"If you would be willing to respond to my letter, I'd be

*honored to continue our correspondence to see if we are a
suitable match.*

"Sincerely,

"Ben Montgomery"

Everly couldn't put the letter down. She read it over
again just to be sure she'd read all of the words correctly.
He sounded almost too good to be true, and that set off
alarm bells in her head. How could she know he was
being truthful?

But for some reason, as she read it for the third time,
her mind recognized the sincerity in the words, and
sensed that he was in as much of a difficult situation as
she was. He wasn't making flowery promises and he
seemed to be genuine in his intentions.

"Well! What did he say?"

Sarah grabbed the letter from her hands before she
could stop her, and as Beth walked in the room, she read
the words out loud.

She could see Beth watching her intently to sense her
reaction to the letter, so she did her best not to give
anything away. Her emotions were jumbled into a
mixture of feelings she didn't understand.

Deciding the best way to react was to show indiffer-
ence, Everly calmly took the letter back from Sarah and
folded it up, placing it in the pocket of her apron.

"He sounds nice, Everly," Beth said.

"Nice? He sounds wonderful!" Sarah exclaimed while
grabbing both of Everly's shoulders in her hands and
pulling her in for a joyous hug. As she stepped back, she
moved her hands down and took Everly's in her own,
while looking in her eyes.

"What are you going to do? Are you going to reply?"

"I don't know yet. I need some time to think." Everly

took her hands from her sister's grip and walked over to the chair to sit down. "I honestly didn't think he'd reply to my letter after I sent it. I know it wasn't the most romantic letter I could have written, and I actually thought it would scare him off. Now I need to figure out what to do."

Deep down, she already knew. Something was pulling her to this stranger that she just couldn't figure out. She sensed, even without meeting him, that he was someone she could possibly come to trust. That was something she'd never been able to give to many people in her life, and especially not a man.

What was it about him that seemed to be different? And how could she be thinking this way without ever having met him?

※

"HELLO, Mr. McConnell. Would you like to come in for a cup of tea?" Everly asked as she opened the door. "Mama is just downstairs making supper for the guests, but she should be home soon."

"That's OK, dear, I'm actually here to see you, but I'd like your mother to be here as well. We can wait until she gets home. And I would love a cup of tea!"

Having known him her whole life, Everly thought Alistair McConnell was likely one of the only men she'd ever really been able to trust and care for. He had always looked out for them, and over the years, had often stopped by to take them all out for some fun.

In truth, she'd suspected that he might have been a bit more interested in her mother than he let on, but because he was so loyal to his friend, he'd never acted on his feelings.

She could sense his nervousness as he paced around the room before speaking. "Have you thought about what you will do, Everly, about the circumstances of your father's will?" He stopped pacing and looked directly at her.

"I know what I have to do, and I've accepted that. Now it's just a matter of finding someone suitable and willing," Everly said slowly. "My family is all that matters to me. I don't want my sisters to worry about having to live a life of poverty at the mercy of any man who decides to take advantage of them." She walked over and set a cup of tea on the table. She turned back to get some cream.

"The problem has been that most men around here know my mother's past and believe that makes me fair game for the same life. It's hard to make a new start with our past always coming up."

Mr. McConnell looked at her with sympathy and nodded his understanding as he came over and sat down at the table.

"I replied to an ad as a mail order bride for a man in Wyoming," she blurted out.

As she said the words, Mr. McConnell began to sputter on the hot tea that was just meeting his lips.

"You did what?" He coughed the words out, then had to set his cup back down as he tried to regain his composure.

"Please, don't tell Mama yet. I didn't think he would actually reply. I wrote it more on a whim to keep Sarah from harping on me about it. When I wrote it, I was very open about the fact I was not looking for marriage for love." She gave him a pleading look as she told him what she had done.

"And he wrote back?"

"I got a letter back yesterday. He seems very nice but I don't know how much I can trust he's even being truthful." Everly had read the letter so many times she almost had it memorized. Each time she tried to find some fault in his words to warrant her distrust, but she hadn't found any yet.

"Can I see the letter?"

She pulled it out of her pocket where she'd kept it close. Her hands shook as she handed it to him.

As he read the letter, she watched his face closely to see if she could get a sense of what he was thinking.

"I can try to check him out if that would help to ease your worries. No promises that I will be able to find much out, but I can do my best. I wouldn't feel comfortable letting you head out to meet, and possibly marry, a man who might be a low-life scoundrel." Everly knew that no matter what she said, he was already planning to do a check on him. She smiled to herself as she felt his concern for her.

"Just promise me you won't say anything to Mama. I don't want her worrying, and until I really know what I will do, there's no sense in her knowing. I plan on writing back to him, and we'll see if he even responds again. Remember, I don't have a whole lot of time, and each letter takes a few weeks to get back. So I need to write soon."

At that, Caroline walked through the door. Everly watched the look on Mr. McConnell's face soften as he saw her, while he stood up to say hello.

"Is there something wrong, Alistair? You and Everly seemed to be talking about something rather dire when I walked in," she joked. Everly watched her mother sit down and noted how tired she looked. She hopped up to pour some tea for her mother.

"Well, I do have a matter I need to discuss with both of you, and I'm not sure how to tell it. I feel like the bearer of such bad news lately and I wish more than anything I had more control over all of it."

Everly carefully set the tea in front of her mother as she sat back down, wary of what he was going to tell them. "What's wrong, Mr. McConnell? Is it about my father's will?"

"I'm afraid so. As you both are aware, your father left behind a wife and a stepson from her first marriage. They've been in to my office and been told about the circumstances of your father's will in regards to how the money will be shared." She noticed that Mr. McConnell couldn't lift his eyes to meet theirs.

"I assume she wasn't happy with the news," Caroline calmly stated.

"To say she was not happy is a bit of an understatement." He finally lifted his eyes from his cup and looked towards them. "She said in no uncertain terms that she would fight the will, and make sure that her name is not associated with your family in any way. That includes making sure no one besides herself gets a cent from Thomas' estate."

Everly jumped from her chair. "Can she fight the will? Can she stop Mama from getting any money? What if I go ahead and get married, then she ends up fighting us and winning? I will have gotten married for nothing!" Everly felt like her head was spinning as all the questions started bubbling to the surface. She was not going to let her mother, or her sisters be left with nothing to support them.

Mr. McConnell stood, and walked over to Everly. He took her hands in his. "Everly, just calm down. I'll do my best to make sure she doesn't fight anything. I'm sure she was just angry after everything she's been through, and then finding out the terms of the will just set her off. She's had to live with the lies and embarrassment your father put her through during their years of marriage as well, and I truly believe she'd hoped now it would just be over. I'm sure once she has a chance to clear her head, she will be a bit more reasonable."

Everly could understand how she must feel as the wife who'd been betrayed for so many years, but she had to focus on making sure her own family was looked after. If this woman was going to cause problems, she better be prepared for a fight. Everly wouldn't let her family suffer any more for what her father had done to them.

CHAPTER 7

Ben opened the letter he'd picked up in town this morning. He hadn't wanted to seem too anxious, especially in front of Hazel who'd handed him his mail. She already seemed suspicious of the fact that he was receiving another letter from someone in Chicago, and he was sure she knew something was going on. As much as he wanted to wave the letter in her face and let her know that she hadn't won, he didn't want to give her the chance to do anything to sabotage what he was planning.

The kids were already in bed, so he finally had some time to himself. Sitting on the front porch, he breathed in the freshness of the evening air. He was so proud of the home he had built for himself, and now his sister's children.

"Dear Ben,

"Thank you for your reply. I truly hadn't expected to hear back from you but was glad to receive your letter. As you have

likely figured out about me, I am not a flowery romantic type of girl, so finding the words to say can be difficult.

"I appreciate the love I can sense you feel for your nieces, and I can understand your need to make sure they are well looked after. I have two younger sisters, and they are my motivation for marrying as well, to ensure they have a better chance for their futures.

"You will not have to provide for them. They will receive money from my father's will at the time of my marriage, so do not feel any pressure or obligation that you'll also be caring for my family if we do marry.

"My twenty-first birthday is now just over two months away, so in truth I feel some pressure to meet you and make sure we are suited for marriage. I can't see myself marrying someone I've only just met, so if it is something you are agreeable to, perhaps we could spend some time together. I would like to meet your nieces and take some time for you and me to learn more about each other.

"We would still need to marry fairly quickly, but at least if we have a few days to spend together first, we can hopefully build a foundation for our future together.

"Again, I apologize for my lack of poetic words. I've never known how to be coy or romantic. I've spent my life trying to keep men from hurting my family, and giving trust or love to a man is not something I take lightly.

"I wish I could offer you more of what I am sure you deserve, as you sound like a very caring man who loves his family. Maybe over time, I could be the kind of wife that could give you more, but I feel it is only fair to make sure you know what you are getting if you choose to marry me.

"I hope to hear from you again soon.

"Sincerely,

"Everly Wilder"

The quiet of the evening was broken by Jake. Ben hadn't even heard him ride into the yard.

"What are you grinning at?" Jake asked as he climbed the steps to the porch and sat down in the chair beside Ben.

"I honestly don't know what to think of this woman. She's not at all what I would've thought I wanted in a wife, but there's just something about her words that draws me to her! She couldn't be more blunt if she came right out and said she hated men and never wanted to marry, yet she seems like...beneath all of that exterior...something I can't quite put my finger on. Something that makes her seem so vulnerable."

Ben held out his hand with the latest letter he'd received from Everly. Jake took it from him and slowly read it. He wasn't sure he agreed with Ben. In fact, she seemed like the last woman in the world he would have chosen as a wife for his cousin. However, the look on Ben's face when he finished reading caused him to put his eyes back to the letter to read again, wondering if he'd missed something Ben had seen.

"Well, I guess you better decide." He handed the letter back to Ben, and leaned back in the chair, crossing his legs at his ankles. "I think the sooner the better. Hazel isn't letting this go. I was in town with your father today while he made arrangements for the horses he'd purchased from Chicago to be brought out. She said to let you know that she was talking with some members of the church about what to do in regards to the living situation out here with the girls."

Ben looked out across the fields. He knew Hazel wasn't the type to give up. He wondered why she hadn't said anything to him herself this morning.

Jake continued as he sat forward in his chair. "You

know what your father is like. He told her to mind her own business and to go find someone else to meddle with. He dared her to keep trying to force your hand into marrying her daughter, which I'm sure will only make things worse."

Ben inwardly cringed as he imagined exactly how his father would have reacted. His dad didn't mince his words, and Hazel likely wouldn't have been too happy with that message. But he also knew his father was not going to bend over and let anything happen to Ben or his granddaughters, so he was grateful to know he had him on his side.

He looked back at the letter he was holding in his hands. "I think the sooner I get Everly out here, the faster I'll get that meddlesome woman out of my life. I've already lost my sister − no one will take these girls from me!"

CHAPTER 8

Everly sat on her bed and looked out the window. This would be her last night in the room she'd shared with her sisters for as long as she could remember. As she watched the people walking on the street below, she thought about everything that had happened over the past few weeks.

She'd received a letter back from Ben containing money for a ticket for her and an escort if she chose to bring one with her. The fact that he'd thought she might like to have a familiar face go with her when she boarded the train to go west, made her think of the kind of man he must be.

He had to have his own misgivings about sending money to a stranger and wondering if she would just use it for herself and he'd never hear from her again. But he'd sent it anyway. And even sent enough for her to bring her mother or one of her sisters along with her.

As she put the last of her things into her small bag, she looked around her room. Her family had never had a lot of frilly things, or the finest of items in their home, but her mother had always made sure they were never hungry or that they didn't feel loved.

She'd never cared about what others thought, but she found herself wondering what Ben would think when he saw her get off the train, carrying her small bag full of everything she owned. Would he think he'd made a horrible mistake, and that she was just after his money?

She would have to tell him the truth about why she was marrying him at some point, but she hoped he'd understand her situation. She'd told him part of the truth. The part about her mother's past wasn't something she had wanted to bring up yet.

She saw Sarah and Beth walking up the street, carrying something in their arms. They looked so excited and happy. She smiled to herself as she watched them, feeling an ache of loneliness knowing she was leaving her life here with them behind. But knowing they'd be happy, and have a chance for more in their lives, also gave her a sense of peace with what she had to do.

She couldn't quite make out what they were carrying, but she was sure she was about to find out.

"Everly! Close your eyes!" Sarah shouted as the girls came through the door.

"What have you two been up to?" she asked, smiling as she closed her eyes.

She could hear some rustling of papers and could tell they were putting something on the bed.

"Open your eyes!"

As Everly opened her eyes, the first thing she noticed was the look of pure happiness on both of her sister's faces. She looked down toward the bed and saw the most beautiful dress she'd ever seen lying beside her packed bag.

The fabric was a silky looking violet with black lace

trim. The bodice scooped down, revealing more black lace accenting below. The skirt seemed to have more folds of fabric than anything she'd ever seen before, and as she looked at it, her hand reached out to stroke the softness.

"It's for you, Everly." Beth looked so young, eagerly waiting to see her reaction to the gift they were giving her.

She looked back down at the dress, gently caressing the luxurious fabric, as she felt tears begin to spill over.

Sarah walked over and put her hand on her shoulder. "We saved up some money from doing small jobs around here. And Mama had some money put away she said for us to use. You've always done so much for all of us and made so many sacrifices to make sure we always had everything we wanted. Now you're heading out towards a new life, one you never had a chance to choose for yourself. And you're doing it all just to make sure we are looked after."

"We thought it was your turn to have something for yourself," Beth added. "When you meet your new husband, we want you to look your best!" Her voice broke, and she coughed to cover the sound.

Everly knew if she tried to speak, the words would be cut short because of the lump in her own throat that was trying so hard to stop her tears. As she reached out her arms, and the younger sisters raced into her embrace, she knew without question that she was doing the right thing. She could get on that train in the morning knowing these girls, who were quickly becoming women themselves, would have their best chance at a better life.

THE TRAIN'S whistle cut through the air, the sound slicing through her thoughts and jarring her ears. Everly had never noticed how loud it was. Maybe she'd just never paid attention to the sound before, never considering the people who were on those trains who might be going somewhere that would change their lives forever.

Today she was one of those people, and as she looked out the window, seeing her mother, Beth and Mr. McConnell standing there on the platform waving, it seemed as though that train whistle was all she could hear. Everything else around her was a quiet hum, and it felt as though everything was moving slower than usual.

Saying goodbye had been so hard. Mr. McConnell had reported to her that the background check on Ben had come back clean. He seemed to be an upstanding and honorable man, but he'd also assured her that he'd be coming out to check for himself very soon.

She tried not to notice the tears on her mother's face, or the strangers walking behind on the platform, going on with their lives as though nothing was out of the ordinary. How could they not understand the monumental moment that was taking place right there in front of them?

She looked at Sarah as the train picked up speed and pulled away from the station. Her sister had been so excited to come with her, and the joy on her face almost made Everly smile despite the ache she was feeling in her heart.

There was no turning back now. In just a few short hours, she'd be in Wyoming, getting ready for her new life with a man who was a stranger. She couldn't believe how much her life had changed in just a few short weeks.

As though she sensed the panic her sister was beginning to feel, Sarah reached out her hand and took Everly's, gripping it tightly while she gave a gentle squeeze. She looked at Everly and offered her a quiet smile.

"Thank you for coming with me, Sarah. I think it's about time we had some adventure in our lives." She tried to show a brave front despite the worry she was actually feeling.

She looked back out the window as the last of the Chicago skyline went out of her view.

❧❦

BEN SAT IN THE WAGON, patiently trying to answer all the questions the girls were throwing at him.

"What color is her hair? How will you know it's her?"

"Will she be bringing us a present?"

"What if she doesn't know how to cook?"

He tried to get them to slow down and give him a chance to answer.

"I think her hair is dark, but I don't know if she ever actually mentioned that or if it's just how I imagine her to be. I guess I'll know it's her because there won't likely be many other people getting off the train in High Ridge, so two women getting off should be fairly easy to spot." He tried to remember everything they'd asked him so he could keep his mind off the fact he was about to meet the woman he might marry.

"No, she won't be bringing you any presents. She is moving halfway across the country to come and take care of all of us, so she doesn't need to be giving you little chickens anything more than that. And, if she can't cook, you'll both just have to teach her how." He joked with the girls, hoping the questions would stop. His nerves were already stretched far, and he was doing his best to act like he had everything under control.

He hadn't wanted to bring the girls, but they were adamant they were coming with him when they heard him and Mary talking in the kitchen yesterday. He figured meeting them might help to ease some of the awkwardness on the ride back to the farm anyway, so he'd agreed to bring them. He was seriously beginning to regret that decision now as they continued to talk, oblivious to the stress he was feeling.

The girls were now arguing about who would get to sit beside her, and as he was about to explain that she'd be sitting up front with him, they all heard the whistle of the train as it came around the bend into town.

What he hadn't noticed was Hazel Hayes, standing outside the store watching. She knew Ben was up to something when he'd come to town with both girls, then headed straight past the store towards the train station at the edge of town. She'd been outside sweeping the step, and now she watched as the three of them hopped down off the buggy and walked toward the train that was slowly pulling up to the platform.

CHAPTER 9

Everly held her head high as she stepped off the train. She was a bundle of nerves, and her sister wasn't helping. Sarah was talking and chattering about how wonderful everything was, how much fun she was having and how she wondered just what the next few days would be like. It was almost more than she could listen to as she stepped onto the platform and looked around at the town that would now be her home.

It was small and dusty. That was what she noticed first. The buildings were not as big or close together as they were in Chicago, but everything looked to be well looked after. There was a small church, a general store and a couple other buildings lining the street. It was not at all what she was used to seeing, but something about it made her feel a sense of comfort.

She could hear children talking amid the chaos of the few people milling around who either were getting off or on the train. She turned her head as she heard a small voice saying, "Do you think that's her?"

She smiled at the young girl with curls who'd spoken,

and then looked up, locking eyes with the man who was standing beside her holding her hand.

There was no doubt in her mind that she was looking at the man who was going to be her husband. Her heart felt like it was doing a somersault in her body, a feeling she'd never felt before in her life. It had to be a combination of nerves and exhaustion, because surely the man she was looking at couldn't have this kind of effect on her already.

His eyes were the darkest blue she'd ever seen, and they seemed to look right into her soul. As he looked at her, he smiled, and she got the feeling that he was used to getting his way with that smile. He had a ruggedness that also made her think that you wouldn't want to cross him.

His hat was pulled down to block the sun, but she could see tufts of dark hair poking out from the sides. He wasn't completely clean shaven, but there wasn't a beard either. Just a growth of dark hair that hinted at a dimple as he smiled.

As she stood there staring, her legs suddenly felt like lead, and Sarah walked right into the back of her, unaware of the situation that was unfolding between the couple looking at each other for the first time. Everly felt herself starting to fall forwards toward the edge of the platform, when strong arms went around her and grabbed her before she could tumble into the dirt.

"Are you all right?" the man's voice was deep, and she could feel his chest rumble as he spoke. She could smell soap as he held her in his arms.

She felt her face start to burn. What a way to make a first impression! She wanted to glare at her sister to let her know how mad she was, but she couldn't seem to tear her eyes away from the eyes that were now just inches from her face.

She was becoming one of those silly swooning girls she despised so much. She knew she had to somehow pull herself together before she made an even bigger fool of herself.

"Yes, I'm fine. Thank you." She spoke with a seriousness that she wasn't really feeling. Her voice sounded strained in her ears, and as she wiped the dust from the front of her dress, she backed away from the man. His hands let her go, and she took a few seconds to compose herself while she busied herself with brushing off her dress.

"Are you Miss Wilder?" She heard the same small voice she'd heard when she first stepped off the train.

She lifted her eyes to the girl who'd spoken and found herself looking into eyes that were the same dark blue as the man beside her.

She decided to bend down and meet the girls eye to eye. "Yes, I am, but you can call me Everly."

The two girls looked at each other with a smile, then threw themselves at her with their arms outstretched. She'd barely recovered her balance, so she could feel herself being thrown backwards as the girls both hugged her with a fierceness she immediately understood. She knew these girls loved their uncle, but they were also missing having a woman who loved them. It was the same way she and her sisters had always felt about having a man who would love them like a father.

Everly felt arms reaching out to steady her again, just as she was sure she would end up on her backside on the platform. This was not the meeting she had imagined in her mind. By now, he must be thinking she was completely unstable and wondering what he'd got himself into by agreeing to send for her.

"Girls! Step back and give Miss Wilder some space.

I'm so sorry, I told them to be respectful and not to over-whelm you too much before you had a chance to settle. I guess they were just too excited to control themselves. Are you all right?" His hands were around her waist, helping her to her feet.

She had to smile despite the seriousness of the situation. She had played the moment of meeting her future husband over in her mind many times, but never had she thought she would have almost fallen not just once, but twice, before they had even introduced themselves to each other.

"You must be Ben." She put her hand out toward him, and felt his hands drop from her sides as he reached his own out. "It's nice to finally meet you." Her voice sounded strange in her ears, as she tried to show a confidence she was not truly feeling.

She could see his dimple again as he smiled, only inches away from her face. She realized how formal she sounded, and was sure he was smiling at her seriousness, especially considering how clumsy she'd appeared since stepping off of the train.

"Nice to meet you too, Everly." He took her hand in his and raised it to his lips for a gently laid kiss. His eyes never left hers, even after she pulled her hand back as though it had been burned.

Their gazes locked, and she was sure now she was suffering ill effects from the train ride. She'd never been one to believe in love at first sight or any of the other silly notions that other girls she knew had spoken of. But she couldn't deny she was feeling twinges of something she'd never felt before, and she knew that had never been part of the plan.

She knew that the men who seemed the most charming, were usually the ones you needed to watch out for more than any others.

She felt a gentle nudge from behind her, and realized she'd completely forgotten about her sister who'd been standing there watching the whole unceremonious meeting between them.

"Oh, and this is my sister Sarah. Sarah, this is Ben," She could tell from her sister's face that she was enjoying this whole situation immensely. She stepped back so Ben and Sarah could meet. He raised Sarah's hand to place a kiss on the back of her hand too, but she noticed he didn't linger as he had with hers.

"I'm Olivia", the young girl with the curls stated, innocently unaware of the sparks that were already starting to fly between the couple before them. "And this is my sister, Elizabeth. She's shy."

Everly crouched down, making sure she had her balance completely this time in case they decided to launch themselves at her again. She put her hand out to each of the girls and smiled at them as they took turns shaking it.

She reached into her bag and pulled out a candy stick for each of them. It wasn't much, but she'd known as a child, small gifts could sometimes mean so much.

"I wanted to bring you something from Chicago. I used to eat these all the time when I was just a little girl, so I thought maybe you girls would like to try them too."

She almost cried at the joy she saw in their eyes. They'd known so much tragedy already in their young lives, and it broke her heart. She stood back up and looked at Ben. His face was soft as he looked at the girls, then back to her.

"What do you say, girls?" he asked them as he kept his eyes on Everly. She couldn't move her own eyes from his, and she could sense the thankfulness he felt at seeing how happy she had made his nieces.

"Thank you!" Both girls squealed as they turned and hopped into the back of the wagon.

Ben reached down for their bags, lifting them with ease. He set them into the back of the wagon with the girls, then reached his hand out to help them down off the platform. It was such a simple act, yet it was one both of them noticed as neither had known much chivalry from men in their lives.

After he'd helped them into the wagon, Everly felt his eyes on her again as he settled into the seat next to her. She looked into his eyes, and he gave her a smile that sent a jolt straight to her heart.

She was going to have to be very careful around this man.

CHAPTER 10

T he wagon ride back to the farm had given Everly the time to regain her composure after her rather unflattering first impression. The girls chatted nonstop, pointing out every building in town, then every house along the way, even every little spot that to them was important. They were most excited to show the creek on the other side of the trees where they sometimes stopped for a picnic on their way home from church on Sundays.

Ben hadn't said much, but she'd caught him glancing her way more than once. She wondered what he was thinking. She'd never imagined she would care what a man thought of her, but for some reason, she hoped he wasn't disappointed in his decision to send for her.

"Just over this hill is the start of our land. Together with my cousin Jake and my father, who also lives on the property, we raise cattle and breed horses. We haven't had a woman living out here for many years now, so I hope you can forgive the lack of more 'feminine' luxuries. When we heard you were coming, we tried to spruce things up a bit, but I fear we are still fairly rough around the edges."

"I am sure it will be lovely, Mr. Montgomery," Sarah gushed. She'd been in awe since she stepped off the train at the beauty around her, and Everly had to smile to see how happy her sister seemed to be in this environment. She had to admit, there was something out here that made her feel a sense of peace and happiness, something she hadn't felt for a very long time, if ever.

"Please call me Ben. You will soon be my sister after all," he winked at her.

Everly could feel her face burning, as Ben and Sarah smiled at each other with a teasing look. She guessed from his comment, he must at least be considering going through with the marriage. Even though she still wasn't happy about what she was being forced to do, she was secretly a bit relieved. She just wasn't sure what was making her feel that way.

As they came around a bend on the road, a house tucked neatly in among some trees came into view. In the midst of miles and miles of green grass all around, to one side there appeared to be hundreds of cows grazing. To the other side of the house, the most beautiful horses Everly had ever seen frolicked and ran in the morning sunlight.

"Ladies, here we are. The most beautiful spot in all of Wyoming."

Everly had to agree. She'd never seen anywhere so beautiful in all her life. She had grown up with hustle and bustle all around her, horses' hooves making sounds on the roads at all times of day. People shouting and talking, dust always in the air and endless noises taking away any chance for quiet.

What lay before her was breathtaking. A small creek

ran through the property, and she was sure she could hear it trickling as they rode by. Birds were chirping in the trees, and an overwhelming peace coursed through her body.

Everly looked at Ben and noticed the smile as he looked with pride at what was laid out before them. For a moment, she could see a man who understood the meaning of hard work and responsibilities, so different from what she'd seen from other men she had known in her life. As she looked back toward the house, she felt a bubbling of excitement as she realized she was looking at what now would be her home.

While she took it all in, an older woman came running through the front door and down the steps before the wagon could even come to a stop.

"Oh, will ye look at the wonderful sight! You ladies must be starved through to yer bones! I've made up some stew to fill you up!" The woman had rosy red cheeks and looked like she had never stopped smiling in her life.

"Mary, let's give the ladies a moment to get themselves settled before you start fussing over them," Ben gently teased the woman.

"This is Mary O'Hara, the wonderful lady who stepped in to help me with the house and the kids when they came to live with me. She lives on a farm just up the road. Mary, this is Everly."

Ben had helped her down from the wagon, and she now stood before the woman who was smiling right down to her toes.

"Oh bless ye dear, ye are a sight for sore eyes! You must be exhausted, and here I am already jumpin' in and fussin' on ye!" Mary spoke with a distinct Irish burr, but was easy to understand even at the rapid rate the words were coming from her mouth.

Everly smiled and reached out her hand as Mary grabbed it in both of hers, then pulled her in for a hug. Caught off guard, Everly wasn't sure how to react, but something about this woman made her feel like she would take care of anyone she cared about, and that already included her. For the first time since stepping on the train, she let herself feel the loneliness she felt for her own mother take over, while she let the woman embrace her.

Stepping back, and still holding her with outstretched arms, Mary looked her up and down. "Aye and ye are a real beauty. Welcome to Wyoming, Everly! You can call me Mary."

Realizing she'd still never even had a chance to say a word, Everly nodded her head, trying to come up with the right words. "It's wonderful to meet you Mary. Ben has spoken of you in his letters. You've done such a good job of caring for this family when they needed you. I hope you can show me what I need to learn to manage a home on my own out here."

"Oh my dear, ye'll have no trouble at all! I can see a strength in ye already that I do not see in many young ladies around here, that's the truth!" Mary squeezed her shoulders, then turned to meet Sarah.

After Sarah was introduced and welcomed by Mary, Ben grabbed the bags and helped them up onto the porch. From what she'd seen so far, there weren't many touches that showed a woman's presence. She guessed that Mary had her own home to tend as well as Ben's, so she wouldn't have had time to worry about flowers or other more feminine aspects while feeding and caring for the family.

When they walked in the door, the smell of the cooking stew filled the air. The kitchen was immaculate, with a vase of flowers on the table covered with an embroidered linen tablecloth.

"I tried to make the place homey for ye when ye arrived, dear."

Everly almost felt a tear escape at the happiness on the woman's face, so desperate to make her feel welcome. She knew that things would be less "civilized" than what Everly was used to but had tried her best to make her feel at home.

"It's lovely, Mary, and I can't tell you how much I appreciate how welcome you've made us both feel. Thank you."

The grin on the woman's face shone with pride at hearing those words. Ben took Everly's arm and led her through the house to the small staircase at the back. Just off the stairs, a door led to a small bedroom that had a comfortable looking bed and small night table with a lamp.

"You can stay here, Sarah, while you're with us," Ben said as he set her bag down by the bed. "There's a room just next door where you can get freshened up before we have something to eat."

Ben looked uncomfortable as he turned back to pick up Everly's bag. He was having trouble looking her in the eye, and she realized that now she'd be finding out her own sleeping arrangements. Ben led the way up the staircase, while she nervously followed.

"There are two rooms up here. The girls share this one on the right, and this room is mine. You can stay here." Ben opened the door and showed a nice sized room, complete with a mirror and washstand next to the bed.

Feeling quite uncomfortable and unsure of what the sleeping arrangements would be, this was the moment

Everly had been dreading since she'd agreed to come out here to meet Ben. She knew it wasn't appropriate for a single woman to be sleeping in a house with an unmarried man, and since she wasn't sure when or even if they were getting married for sure, the entire situation caused her to unconsciously rub her hands together while looking away from Ben.

Sensing her discomfort, Ben set her bag down and turned back towards where she was still standing in the doorway. He was finally able to look her in the eye, so she knew he was just as uncomfortable as she was.

"I'll be sleeping in the room we have in the barn until we're married." Blushing, he added, "That is, if you're still agreeable to marriage after staying here for a while."

Everly felt the breath she didn't even know she'd been holding rush from her lungs. "Thank you. Your room looks very nice. I'm sure I will be comfortable." Unsure of what else to say, or what to do to help break the seriousness of the moment, she walked toward her bag and started to open it.

"I'll leave you to get freshened up. Whenever you're ready, you can come back down, and we can have a bite to eat. Maybe after lunch I can take you around the property a bit and show you some more."

"Thank you, I'd like that."

She watched his back as he turned to leave, and she noticed the smile he had on his face. She was relieved that he'd understood her discomfort and had taken the time to make arrangements to protect her reputation. He'd also understood her need for time to get more comfortable with him before getting married.

She still couldn't let herself believe there wasn't more to Ben Montgomery than he was letting on, but she had no choice now but to continue on and hope they would make a good match. She had no more time. Her twenty-first birthday was in just one month now and finding another man to marry before then would be impossible. If she didn't marry Ben, her family would be left with nothing, and she was determined not to let that happen.

CHAPTER 11

Ben sat on the porch and replayed the day in his mind. When he first saw her step off the train, he'd known exactly which one was Everly. The way she held her head, even while her eyes betrayed the fear she was feeling, left no doubt in his mind who she was. The dress she was wearing made her eyes stand out, and her gaze had reached across the platform and pierced straight into his heart.

He knew she must have been exhausted from the trip and worried about her future in a strange place, but the way she carried herself gave none of that away.

As she'd looked towards him, Ben had felt a shock course through his body. He didn't quite know what had happened, but he could sense a pull towards her. He knew the exact moment she'd spotted him, and hoping to make the best impression he could, he'd started to take a step forward when he saw the lady behind her bump into her, knocking her forward.

He'd grabbed her arm to steady her, then while he

looked into her eyes, he somehow knew he had to convince this woman to stay.

His thoughts were interrupted by the sound of hooves coming up the lane beside the house. He watched Jake ride up next to the porch where he was sitting and hop off his horse.

"So, do I get to meet her?" he asked as he sat down beside Ben.

Before the words were even out, the door opened, and he could see the expression on Ben's face instantly soften into a smile. He turned toward the door and realized what Ben was smiling at.

"Ben," Everly said, "the girls were hoping Sarah and I could read them a story before bed, so we'll just get them tucked in and call you when they're ready for you to say goodnight, if that's all right."

Both men stood when she came through the door, and Ben introduced her to Jake. He didn't want to admit it, but he cared what Jake thought of her, so he watched his face closely to see his expression. As usual, Jake didn't give anything away, but as Everly turned to go back in the house, he could see the grin on his cousin's face as he looked back at him.

"How did an ugly old goat like you ever convince a woman like her to come out here for you?" he teased.

"Well, if I'm an old goat I shudder to think what that makes you," Ben threw back.

The two of them had practically grown up together and were more like brothers than cousins. They often sat together in the evening and good-natured teasing was nothing out of the ordinary.

Jake sat quietly for a minute looking out at the fields. "Something must be wrong with her. Why would she ever agree to come all the way out here to meet a man she's never met, and even agree to marry, if there wasn't something stopping her from finding a man on her own back home?"

"I told you, Jake, she has some kind of obligation to marry before her twenty-first birthday next month," Ben reminded him. He hoped Jake would just leave it alone, but he should have known his cousin wouldn't remain quiet.

Jake sat forward in his chair and put his arms on his knees. "You mean she still hasn't told you why? How can you trust her? You have to be careful, Ben. You have those girls to consider now and letting a stranger in for them to get attached to without knowing everything you can about her is dangerous."

Ben knew that and had thought it himself many times. How could he explain that something made him feel she could be trusted? That she needed him as badly as he needed her, and that he sensed something they shared in common...trying to do what they had to do to ensure the people they loved were taken care of.

"Especially when I tell you that Hazel was snooping around and asking questions today after she saw you at the train picking two women up."

Ben stood and ran his fingers through his hair. He knew she'd likely seen them but hoped he could get out of town without raising too many suspicions. If Hazel Hayes knew what he was doing, she'd do everything in her power to stop it. He had no doubt about that.

"What did she say?"

"She wasted no time confronting me when I went into the store this afternoon. Said she'd noticed you at the train station with your nieces picking two women up. She demanded to know who they were."

Jake grinned as he remembered the confrontation.

"Of course, I left her with even more questions as I played it up and pretended I had no idea of who it could be. I told her you had never mentioned anything to me at all, and that maybe you'd gone off and got yourself married when you took that trip for cattle last month."

Ben groaned while he listened to Jake chuckle about the reaction Hazel had when he'd said that to her.

"Why would you say that to her? You know it will only rile her up more, and she'll most likely be showing up on my doorstep now to find out what's really going on! I should have known she wouldn't let this go." Ben paced in front of the steps, trying to think of what he could say when she did show up.

"Oh, Ben, lighten up. You have Everly here now, and there really isn't much Hazel can do anyway to stop you from marrying her. And her followers will get tired of it all once they see that they have nothing to grumble about anymore," Jake assured him.

Ben stopped pacing and turned towards Jake. "I still have to convince her to actually marry me, Jake, or have you forgotten that part? She's only here on the agreement to see if we are suitable for marriage. She hasn't come right out and agreed yet. Hazel might be able to wiggle her way in yet if I'm not careful."

With that, the door opened, and Sarah walked out to let Ben know that the girls were ready for him to come up and finish tucking them in. He almost laughed out loud at the stunned look on Jake's face as he saw the other woman in front of him. Ben had noticed Everly's younger sister was attractive, but in his eyes, she was nowhere near as stunning as the older sister.

He could tell by Jake's reaction that he definitely thought otherwise.

As payback for the comment Jake had made to Hazel

earlier in the day, he decided to introduce them, then leave Jake there to handle himself in front of her on his own.

Walking through the door, he could hear Jake stammering to find something to say, and he almost felt bad for leaving poor Sarah out there to deal with him.

❧

EVERLY HAD BEEN THERE for almost a week, and still felt awestruck whenever she walked onto the front porch and breathed in the air. She was sure there was never a time in her life when she'd felt such contentment.

The girls seemed to have accepted her into their little family already, along with Mary, Jake and even Ben's father who had been around a few times since she arrived. Everyone was so welcoming and seemed genuinely happy for her to be here.

The only one she was having trouble figuring out was Ben. He'd been the perfect gentleman ever since she arrived, and she began to think maybe she'd been wrong in judging all men the same. Ben seemed to prove all her earlier thoughts about how men treated women to be false, and she honestly didn't know what to believe anymore.

Every time she looked at him, it seemed he was looking directly back at her. She was even able to sense when he was watching her, feeling his eyes on her no matter what she was doing. Sometimes she felt he was just as confused about his feelings as she was, as he would divert his eyes before she could catch him.

But other times, he didn't even blink when she looked toward him. It was almost as though he was looking directly into her mind to see if he could figure out what she was thinking. And sometimes, his look was so intense, she almost believed he could.

Like the day his hand had brushed hers while he helped her into the wagon, and he'd just looked down at his hand like it had been scorched. He'd lifted his eyes to hers, and she was sure she could hear his heart beating. She'd held his gaze, unsure of the feelings she was experiencing. She felt like her body was betraying her and was sure her eyes were pleading with him to lower his lips to hers.

She'd thought he was going to, until the girls came racing out the door, breaking the spell that seemed to have them both caught up in it.

Then, last night when they were sitting on the porch after the girls were in bed, Sarah had gotten up to go into bed. She had stood to go too, but Ben had asked her to sit with him a bit longer. Secretly, she'd hoped he was going to ask her what her decision was or let her know what he himself had decided about where they would go from there.

Instead, he'd talked to her about his sister, and how hard it had been to lose her. She learned just how much he loved his nieces and had started to understand why he was so afraid of losing them. He'd shared how much he loved his ranch, and the work he did with the animals. She felt that she had learned so much about this man, and the feelings she was starting to have for him scared her.

When he'd started to ask more about her, she felt her old defenses come up, and she couldn't bring herself to tell him any more than she already had. She was sure if she told him about her mother's past, or how her mother had let a married man keep her while giving birth to three girls out of wedlock, that Ben wouldn't be able to understand. She worried he'd be like so many other men before him who immediately thought that a child of this woman would not be suitable for marriage.

She worried that if he found out about her past, and why she was having to marry, he'd send her back to Chicago. She knew she was tarnished in the eyes of society, and she felt bad for concealing her past, especially when he'd been so open with her.

Her hope was that her past would remain where it was in Chicago and wouldn't follow her out here. Ben never needed to know the whole truth, and she'd make sure that her family history wouldn't affect his life in any way. She'd started to feel like she could truly be happy here, and she was terrified that if her past came out, she would lose everything.

CHAPTER 12

Sundays in High Ridge were a day of rest, church and family. They hadn't been out and about in town since she'd arrived, so this was Everly's first introduction to many of the people in the small community.

Everly wished she could be as relaxed and excited as Sarah was, but she also knew that Sarah didn't have the worry of trying to win over the people of the community she was hoping to make her home. Everly felt the need to make Ben proud, and that thought confused her more than she could understand. Somehow, since she'd showed up in Wyoming, she felt like she'd lost control of her future. She'd known the minute she arrived that this was where she wanted to stay.

Now, she needed to convince Ben that he wanted her to stay too.

As they turned onto the street where the little white church sat, they could see wagons and buggies arriving from every direction. All the women were dressed in their Sunday best, and the atmosphere around the church was happy and relaxed while people waved and shouted hello to those arriving.

Everly felt Ben's hand reach out for hers, and she looked down at their hands while he gave it a gentle squeeze. When she looked up, he was smiling at her, with his eyes twinkling beneath the cover of his hat.

"Are you nervous?"

She looked back around at the people climbing down from the wagons, noticing how the faces were all smiling. She felt a bit more relaxed, and sensed that she was somewhere safe, where people were maybe a little more laid back than what she'd always known.

The wagon came to a stop and she smiled back at Ben. "A little bit, but..." The rest of her answer was cut short by the squealing of both girls as they saw their "Uncle" Jake pull up on his horse beside them.

"Get me down first, Uncle Jake!" Elizabeth shouted.

Jake smiled at the girls, while climbing down from his horse. He reached up and swung Elizabeth out, then grabbed Olivia and twirled her around before setting her down. The girls were both jumping up and down, barely able to contain their excitement at being in town. They were both so excited to show Everly off and introduce her to everyone, they were reaching up telling her to hurry.

Ben had already come around to get Everly, and he held her stare for what seemed like an eternity while he reached his hand up for her. She took his hand, and stood, then gasped as he reached both hands out and swung her down as Jake had done with the girls.

"Ben!" Everly was mortified, knowing that everyone's eyes were on her. Having Ben toss her out of the wagon like a sack of feed was not the first impression she'd planned on making.

Ben just grinned, and any further chastising she might have had for him was lost as the girls each took one of her hands and pulled her forward.

Jake had stayed back to help Sarah out of the carriage. As she was being pulled along, she looked back and saw her sister being tossed out as unceremoniously as she had been. The look on Sarah's face when Jake finally set her down, indicated just how happy she was about it.

Obviously, these cowboys had different ideas of the proper way to treat a lady in public than what they'd seen on the streets of Chicago.

Names became a blur as the girls pulled Everly from one person to the next while they climbed the steps to the church. Ben had followed along, still grinning from ear to ear, pumping hands with the men and accepting pats on the back as though he'd already managed some tremendous feat by getting a woman to come to church with him.

The women had all been kind and seemed genuinely happy to meet her. She already felt like she was being accepted, and had received many invitations for tea, as well as offers to help her adjust to life out west. She looked at Ben and had to smile as she realized he was starting to feel slightly uncomfortable at the attention they were receiving.

As they sat down in their pew, she noticed that Jake and Sarah were left sitting beside each other. She also noticed how neither one of them looked too unhappy about it.

They'd brought a picnic lunch to stop and enjoy on their way back home. The girls had been completely shocked that Everly and Sarah had never been on a picnic, so they'd insisted they stop after church in their special "picnic spot" they liked.

Everly was almost as excited as the girls, and as they hurried down the steps toward the carriage, she didn't notice the woman standing beside it. But she sensed a change in Ben as soon as he saw her, and for reasons she didn't know, she tensed and braced herself for a meeting with someone she immediately knew was not happy to see her.

"Well, Ben, there sure has been a buzz of talk all morning about your lady friend. I heard you had some visitors but wasn't sure who they were as you'd never brought them around the store. My goodness, your nieces seem to be quite taken with her, telling everyone that you're going to marry her." The woman had an air about her, like she felt she was above everyone else. Her words may have been polite, but her demeanor dripped with venom.

Everly could feel Ben vibrating with barely controlled anger as he held his hand on her back. She'd heard enough of Ben's reasons for needing to marry the other night when they'd spoken on the porch to realize instantly this was the Hazel Hayes he had told her about.

She put her hand out graciously toward the woman before Ben could say anything and introduced herself.

"My name is Everly, and I'm sure you must be Mrs. Hayes. Your reputation precedes you, as I've heard so much about you. It's such a pleasure to finally meet you." Everly almost gushed with a sweetness that was immediately obvious to everyone listening she was not truly feeling at all.

Hazel had no option but to extend her hand to Everly, as many people had stopped what they were doing to quietly watch this exchange. Ben was well liked in this community, and many people were not happy with the conniving way Hazel was trying to remove the girls from his care. If not for the few followers Hazel had, who were too afraid to stand up to her themselves, she wouldn't have a leg to stand on. However, she had some powerful connections, and everyone knew that.

"Now, if you'll excuse us," Everly continued, "we're all very excited to be on our way to a family picnic that has been planned for today. I hope you'll understand our need to get on the road so we can share some much needed fun with these girls! Spending time with family who loves them is so important, wouldn't you agree?" Everly gushed with innocence as she said the words.

She was sure she could hear Ben chuckle behind her as she turned her back on Hazel without giving the woman a chance to reply. Noticing the smiles on every-ones' faces around her, she knew she'd made a bitter enemy. However, the satisfaction of seeing the look on Hazel's face as she'd turned to step into the wagon, was worth it.

Ben extended his hand, and graciously helped her up into the wagon. He was much better mannered in getting her in to the wagon than he'd been when taking her out earlier. She caught the hint of a sparkle in his eye she'd never noticed before. As she looked at him, he winked and smiled.

She knew he was happy with how she'd handled that situation, and she felt a pride that she didn't quite under-stand. What was it about this man that caused her to feel like she needed to defend and protect him as much as she'd always done for her sisters? She loved her sisters, so she could understand that. These feelings she was starting to discover towards Ben scared her more than she cared to admit.

As HE GATHERED the rest of the items out of the wagon, Ben inwardly smiled as he replayed the morning in his mind. Everly had met the congregation with grace and ease, even though he could tell how nervous she was. Then, when she had soundly put Hazel in her place while sounding like an angel from heaven, he'd almost laughed out loud.

He knew that now he'd have to be extra careful as far as Hazel was concerned; she wouldn't take even a small public humiliation lightly. But that was a small price to pay to be able to see her face when Everly had turned her back on her.

"Uncle Ben, look how high I am!" Elizabeth shouted from the branch of a tree that jutted out over the creek.

"Elizabeth! Get down from there or you'll fall and break your neck!" Everly raced towards the tree even as the words were coming from her mouth. Ben could see the genuine fear and concern on her face as she ran to the rescue of his niece.

"I don't have to come down, I always climb up here, don't I, Uncle Ben?" Elizabeth pouted. Ben walked up behind where Everly stood at the base of the tree and looked up to where Elizabeth sat on the branch.

"Listen to Everly, Elizabeth. We don't want to worry her, and if she tells you to do something, then you need to obey her." With that, he walked away, leaving both Everly and Elizabeth to stare at his back.

He heard Elizabeth whining that it wasn't fair as she started to climb down. Just when he was almost out of earshot, he heard a rustle of branches and something cracking, followed by a small scream. He whirled back around in time to see Elizabeth laying on the ground, with Everly leaning over her.

As the rest of them ran to help, Ben saw Everly

dabbing at blood on Elizabeth's arm with her dress. The beautiful dress she'd been wearing when she got off the train, the only nice dress she owned. The fact that she didn't care about it as much as she cared about Elizabeth tugged at his heart.

By the time they'd all gathered back around, Elizabeth was sitting up hugging Everly, who was soothing her and wiping at the tears running down her cheeks.

"I just slipped, Uncle Ben, I didn't mean to!" Elizabeth sobbed as Ben crouched down beside them. He put his hand on Everly's back, offering her reassurance as she soothed the crying girl. He could feel her trembling, still scared from seeing Elizabeth fall from the tree.

"I know, Elizabeth, but that's why Everly asked you to get down. We didn't want you to get hurt worse." Ben had always let them do things like climb trees without worrying about the possibility of them getting hurt. He guessed women were more apt to worry, and he should've stayed and helped Elizabeth down from the tree for Everly's sake.

"I'm sorry. Are you mad at me, Everly?" Elizabeth pulled back and looked at Everly's face. The tears were starting to dry, and Ben could see dirt caked on her cheeks from falling on the ground.

"I could never be mad at you, Elizabeth. I'm just so glad you weren't hurt worse!" Everly was still dabbing at the blood on Elizabeth's arm, then reached up and wiped more off by her lip.

"But I ruined your dress." Elizabeth's lip started to quiver again as she looked down at the hem of the dress that now was stained with blood.

"This old thing? I have other dresses, but there's only one you. Now let's get back to the picnic! This is my first one, remember? I need you to show me just how much fun it can be!" Ben knew that Everly was lying, and he made a silent vow to replace her dress with as many as she wanted.

Everly stood up and took Elizabeth's hand to walk back to the opening where they'd set up their picnic. She took Olivia's hand too, noting the worried look she had that her sister might have been hurt badly.

At that moment, watching this woman walk away with the two little girls he loved more than anything, Ben knew that he would do whatever he had to in order to convince Everly she belonged there with them.

CHAPTER 13

The day had turned out perfect, after the rough start. Everly had never had so much fun in her life, and as she'd sat there watching Ben with the girls, she felt a sadness for what she had always yearned for with her own father. She had no fun memories like the kind Ben enjoyed with his nieces. Watching them together helped her to realize this man was not like the man she had grown up hating so much.

She'd watched the girls playing, and had relaxed in the beauty of her surroundings, not worrying about anything for the first time in her life. The day had ended too soon, and they'd come home so the men could do their chores. Everyone had been played out when they got home and could hardly wait to crawl into their beds.

She carried a cup of tea out to where Ben sat on the porch, as he always did in the evening. The girls were all tucked into bed, and Sarah had already retired for the night. She hoped to have a chance to talk to Ben about what their future would be. She'd run out of time, with her birthday coming up already next week. Reminding him about her need to wed before that day caused her to worry it would shatter the happiness that had built up over the day, but she didn't know a way around it.

"The girls are all tucked in, and they were asleep almost before I got out of the room!" Everly smiled at him as she handed Ben his tea and sat in the chair next to him.

She tried to think of a way to bring up the topic of marriage. "They sure had fun today. You're so good to them, and they absolutely adore you. They're lucky girls to have an uncle who cares about them as much as you do." Everly watched Ben as he shifted his legs in the chair, never taking his eyes off the tea she'd handed him.

"Is everything all right? I thought I remembered you liked a bit of milk in with your tea, but I can go back and make another one for you if that isn't right..." She felt so nervous and hopped back up to take the tea from his hands. She was already on edge, and she didn't know how to settle her nerves.

"Everly, it's fine." Ben looked at her, and she almost felt her knees buckle. Between the nerves she was feeling, and the intensity of his gaze when he lifted his eyes to hers, she felt like she was just about to snap.

"I really enjoyed the picnic today. I was so worried after Elizabeth fell that the day would be ruined, but I think everyone had fun. The people in town were all very nice too..." She realized she was stammering when she noticed the corners of Ben's lips curve up into a smile.

She stopped talking and looked down at her hands. She could feel his eyes on her without even looking up, like she always could when he looked at her. Her mouth suddenly felt quite dry, and she wished she'd just gone up to bed without coming out here and embarrassing herself so badly in front of Ben.

"Everly, having you here has been a nice change for all of us. The girls have both grown quite fond of you, as you saw today at church and at the picnic. You're exactly what they need. I know that your birthday is coming up, and you'd said you needed to be married before then, so I guess what I would like to know is whether you've decided we are suitable?"

She sat looking at Ben with a dumbfounded look, wondering if he'd somehow been able to read her thoughts. She also realized he hadn't said anything about his own feelings toward her, but it was a start.

"I have thought about it. Have you?" Suddenly she realized she needed to hear him say that he wanted her to stay. The words came out quietly as she looked into his eyes.

Ben took her hands in his, and she could feel the strength in them as they stopped hers from trembling. "I've thought about nothing else since I first saw you. Hearing you say you want to stay and marry me would make me the happiest man in the world."

It might not have been the most romantic of proposals, but Everly knew it came from his heart. Her heart did somersaults as she looked into his eyes. She worried her legs were about to give out on her.

"I do believe we are well suited, Ben, and I would be happy to marry you. I've grown to love the girls as well as this home you have built here. Wyoming is beautiful and I can see myself making this my home forever." She desperately wanted to say more, to tell him that she'd found herself falling for him too but wasn't ready to leave herself open to his rejection if he didn't feel the same.

Ben smiled, and never moved his eyes from hers. He got out of his chair, then came over, kneeling before her and took her hands in his. "Well then, Everly Wilder, I would like to ask officially for you to be my wife. I know we've not met under normal circumstances, but you are more than I could have ever hoped for. If you will have me, have all of us, I would be honored if you'd marry me – and the sooner the better!"

Everly was sure she was as close to being swept off her feet as she could have ever imagined. Especially since just a few short months ago she'd never felt she would ever trust a man, never mind be making plans to marry him.

She smiled at Ben. "I would be honored to be your wife." With that, Ben stood up, and brought his face closer, gently pressing his lips to hers. She felt a shock go right through from where his lips were touching hers down to her toes. She never wanted him to stop, but he pulled back, and looked at her with a passion that was so raw, she knew she had to get away from him to gather her senses.

"We can tell the girls in the morning. They'll be so happy, I'm sure." She nervously broke the spell saying the first words she could think of.

"I'm sure we all will be." Never taking his eyes from hers, he brought his lips down to hers again. This time, she didn't stop him. He gently caressed her lips with his, while his strong arms wrapped around her. She'd never known a feeling like this. She gasped as he pulled his head back, while his eyes stayed on her lips.

"I don't know what you've done to me, Everly Wilder, but I'm relieved beyond words that you are staying. I hope I can make you as happy as you've made me since the day you stepped off that train." With those words, he set her away from him, then turned and started his walk to the barn. She desperately wanted to beg him to come back, and kiss her some more, but she knew that would be dangerous. She watched him until he was inside the barn, then slowly put her fingers to her lips. She turned and went back in the house, sure that the smile she had on her face would never come off.

⊙⊙⊙

EVERLY COULD FEEL the heat climbing in her cheeks as Ben walked in the door the following morning. His eyes found hers immediately, and she had to avert her eyes and turn back to the oven before he noticed how flushed he was making her.

"Uncle Ben! Everly is making biscuits! I told her they were my favorite, and yours too, right?" Olivia was always so happy in the mornings, and Ben reached down to tousle her hair as he agreed with her that they were his favorite too.

She could feel him behind her before she even had a chance to turn. He bent his head down and quietly whispered good morning in her ear. The shock she felt throughout her body caused her to drop the pan she was holding to set the biscuits in. She was sure the noise could be heard all the way in town, as she hurriedly bent to pick it up and wipe it off.

Ben grinned and walked back to sit down at the table. Both girls jumped into his lap to start telling them everything they had planned for the day. Everly took a few minutes to compose herself again before having to carry the finished breakfast to the table. Mary was still coming to help out, but she hadn't arrived yet, so Everly had decided to make breakfast for the family herself this morning. She was going to have to start taking on her full role here now that she knew she'd be staying.

Sarah had come out from her room, and was now sitting across the table, pouring syrup onto her biscuits. "You always make the best biscuits, Everly. I guess I'll have to get used to making my own if you decide you're staying here..." Sarah quickly glanced towards Everly with an apologetic look for bringing the topic up.

She noticed the girls had still been talking excitedly to Ben, so she wasn't sure if he'd heard. But he lifted his head and smiled at her while he put his hands out in surrender to the girls, telling them he needed a chance to have a word too.

"Elizabeth. Olivia. You both knew that when Everly came out, we hoped she would be someone you could both come to love, and maybe she would decide to stay to help me with raising you. We know she could never replace your ma, who loved you more than words. But you need a woman who can care for you as a mother would. Everly and I talked last night, and she has agreed to stay here with us, and marry me." He smiled up at her as he remembered the moment they'd shared last night.

Before he could add more, the girls both jumped from his lap and ran to Everly with their arms out. "Oh, Everly! I knew you would stay!" Olivia was crying tears of joy that made her heart melt.

"Uncle Ben is a nice man, and he will look after you, I promise!" Elizabeth added.

Everly smiled while she hugged both girls, then set herself back to look them in the eye.

"I'm so happy to be able to stay with all of you. I need you girls to show me everything I need to know how to live out here, so I need you to be my biggest helpers!"

She held her hands on their shoulders as she continued. "I know I will never be your ma, but she would have wanted someone who could love you both and raise you right. I'll do my best to make you all happy." With those last words, she looked up at Ben, who was watching intently.

Sarah, who'd remained quiet knowing Everly needed that moment with the girls, grabbed her into a hug as she stood up. "I'm so happy for you, Everly! I knew this was going to work out!"

Everly laughed as she hugged her back. "Yes, Sarah, somehow you always knew this was what I needed to do. And, as much as it pains me to admit it, you were right."

Among all the commotion, Jake walked in the door, announcing how wonderful breakfast smelled.

"Did I miss something?" he asked as he pulled out a chair and sat down, grabbing a biscuit for himself and putting it onto a plate.

"Well, since I didn't realize we were feeding the entire town this morning, we didn't know we had to wait for you to get here for our announcement," Ben jokingly chided. "Everly has agreed to marry me and stay in High Ridge."

Jake leaped up and patted Ben on the back. "Way to go, old man! How you managed to convince her to stay and put up with you I'll never know, but congratulations."

He turned and grabbed Everly in an embrace. "Welcome to the family! If he ever steps out of line, just let me know and I will tune him in as I've had to do so many times over the years," he joked.

Ben raised an eyebrow as he looked at his cousin. "Is there a reason you decided to join us unannounced for breakfast this morning, or are we just lucky?" Ben sarcastically asked him.

"Ahhh now, Ben. You know you love having me pop in

to visit. However, today I do have a reason, although now I fear it isn't near as exciting as the news you just shared." He went back to lathering jam onto his biscuit, seemingly oblivious to the others in the room who were waiting for him to continue.

"Remember how your dad and I had been looking for someone to partner with back east who was known for his hearty stock? We signed the papers just this morning with our newest partner who has agreed to move west and work with us to grow the most impressive horse breeding ranch this country has ever seen. They should all be arriving to meet you shortly. Just wanted to give you the heads up."

Everly turned back to the oven to put some more biscuits in to make sure there was enough for everyone. She didn't know much about the business Ben did with Jake and his father, so she let them talk about Jake's news among themselves. While she mixed up some more batter, she tried to stop the niggling thoughts that crept in telling her she wasn't being completely honest with Ben about her past, and that she needed to come clean about all of it.

She just didn't know how to tell him, and she knew that since she'd left it so long, now it was going to be even harder. The time seemed like it would never be right. But she knew that even though everything seemed so happy right now, she had to find a way to tell him. It wasn't fair to marry him without him knowing the truth about her mother or how her and her sisters had grown up, even if it meant she would lose it all.

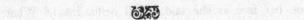

THE SOUND of hooves coming up the road leading to the house broke the celebration that was happening inside the house. Breakfast had been fun, with lots of laughing and listening to Jake talk about what Everly was getting herself into by marrying Ben. Good-natured joking and excited chatter from the kids made for the kind of morning Everly hoped would be the norm once she was settled into her new life.

"There's your dad now, and he's brought our new partner out for you to meet! He brought his mother out this way with him as she is funding some of the new deal as well."

They stood up to go outside, and Everly and Sarah started to clean up the table. "Leave the mess, ladies. I want to share the news of our marriage to dad, so now is as good a time as any!" Ben took the dishes from Everly's hand and laid them on the cupboard beside the table. He took her hand in his and led her out the door.

The dust was starting to settle around the wagon that had stopped in the yard, along with the lone horse and rider that was now dismounting with his back to them. Everly assumed this was the new partner they'd talked about.

When the man turned towards her, she gasped, and her hand flew to cover her mouth. Ben looked at her in shock, then back to the man who was walking toward them, looking just as shocked as Everly had been.

"Everly Wilder? Is that you?" the stranger asked.

Everly felt the world start to spin around her, as she looked toward the wagon and recognized the woman who'd stepped down to the ground. She had a smug look on her face as she said, "Well hello, Everly! What a surprise it is to see you here!"

Everly knew the color had gone from her face, and

she could barely make out the words Ben was saying to her. She looked into Ben's worried eyes and reached out to him.

"Everly! Are you all right?" Those were the last words she heard before she felt her legs give out beneath her, and Ben's strong arms catch her before she hit the ground.

CHAPTER 14

Everly's eyes flickered open, and she could make out Ben's face worriedly hovering over her own. When he saw her waking up, he looked relieved as he bent his head to her hand he was holding while he sat next to the bed.

"I guess they've told you who they are," she quietly said to him.

"No, I haven't gone back down, although I'm sure Jake will have all of the information out of them by now. I assume from your reaction they're not people you were hoping to see out here."

She closed her eyes as the throbbing in her head took over. Why hadn't she just told him the truth? She knew by seeing them here that her past was about to become known to everyone. She should've known she couldn't get away from the truth.

Before she could tell Ben any more, Jake called up the stairs, "You better get down here now, Ben! Hazel just showed up with a couple cronies from town and she's demanding to talk to you!"

Ben ran his hands through his hair. Looking at him now, Everly wanted to cry. How could the morning have started out so perfectly and then fallen apart so badly? She could see her happiness crumbling around her.

She knew he was torn between staying to make sure she was all right and going to see what was happening downstairs.

"You go, Ben. I'll be right down." She almost wept with the sadness that was weighing her down.

Ben cursed, then stood and went out the door. Tears started to well in her eyes as she watched him leave. She sat up and held her head in her hands while she sat on the edge of the bed. Sarah came up then and knelt in front of her.

"Ben told me to come up and make sure you're all right. Oh, Everly! What are we going to do? This is such a mess! Why would daddy's wife and her son need to come here?"

"I never told you, Sarah, because I didn't want to worry you. Before we came out here, Lucy had gone to Mr. McConnell after finding out about the terms of our father's will. She told him she wouldn't let us get anything. After what she'd been put through by him, the humiliation after she couldn't give him a child and knowing he had another woman who had, was more than she could handle, I guess. The son she had before she was widowed was never accepted by our father. She's angry, and I guess she wants to make sure we are punished."

"But how did she know where we are?" Sarah asked.

"I don't know, but I think we need to start packing. We can't stay here now. Ben will be angry at me for not telling him everything. Now that Hazel is here, I'm sure she's found out about our mother, and she will use that information against me. I should have trusted him enough to tell him myself, but it's too late now." With that, she turned and pulled her lone bag out of the closet where it seemed she had put it so long ago. Now she was packing up her few things again, this time knowing she'd let everyone down. And that included the family she'd come to care about here.

❦

BEN RACED DOWN THE STAIRS, the blood boiling in his veins so hot he was having trouble seeing clearly. Seeing Everly's face when she first saw those people had scared him, and when she fell towards the ground, he'd felt like his world was falling with her. He'd never known fear like it before.

He knew these people had something on her that she didn't want to tell him, and he had no doubt that Hazel Hayes was about to make things a whole lot worse for all of them.

"Does someone want to tell me what is going on before I head back inside and grab my gun?" he roared as he threw open the door. He moved down the steps with an agility that left no doubt in anyone's minds how angry he was.

"Who are you?" he strode straight to the man who he believed had started it all. "You better start talking, and it better be the truth because I am in no mood for lies."

"Hold on, man, let me explain! I'm Andrew Barrett. My mother was married to Everly's father. My own father died when I was just a baby, and my mother married Thomas Elliott after that. I was raised by Thomas, but he never treated me as anything more than a hired hand to him, so I have no love for the man. I was just as shocked to see Everly as she was to see me. If you'd given me a second to explain before you threw yourself in my face, you would have noticed that I was asking for answers too." The man looked just as angry as Ben felt.

"I only saw Everly a few times, by accident, as we were never raised together at all. In fact, I don't think we were ever supposed to even know about the other. I have no animosity towards her, and I'm sorry to have caused her such despair on seeing me. I never would've done it on purpose."

The man sent an angry look toward the woman who'd stepped out of the wagon. During it all, the presence of Hazel Hayes had been forgotten, but she wasn't going to stay quiet any longer.

"That's enough small talk, Ben Montgomery. I'm here to get the children. They cannot live in an environment like this, being raised by a woman who was herself raised by a whore." Hazel had the look on her face of someone who'd finally won a hard-fought battle while she walked over to Ben.

Jake saw the cold fury in Ben's face, and he grabbed hold of his arms, holding him back from doing something he may regret.

No one had noticed Everly coming onto the porch, followed by her sister.

"Everly, where are you going?" Elizabeth screamed the words, caught up in fear with such tension all around her. "Don't leave me!" She ran toward Everly and flung herself into her skirts. Ben had forgotten the girls were still there, and he silently chastised himself for not getting them inside sooner.

"Elizabeth. Olivia. Go in the house and wait there. No one is going anywhere until I get some answers."

"No! I'm not leaving her!" By now, Olivia had joined her, and they were both grabbing at Everly's legs, crying and begging her to stay. She'd set the bag down and crouched down to hold the girls in her arms, trying to soothe them and wipe their tears.

Ben looked at Everly and raised an eyebrow as he looked towards her bag. She couldn't bear to look at him, so she nestled her head between the girls she was holding.

Jake let go of Ben, and went to take Elizabeth's hand, pulling her from Everly. Sarah took Olivia, and they went inside the house.

Ben's father, having stood back while the drama unfolded before him, now bellowed into the quiet that had followed the kids going inside. "You'd better start explaining, Andrew Barrett." He walked slowly toward the man he'd just agreed to take on as a partner.

"No, I think my mother had better start explaining. I'm as confused as the rest of you. So, what do you have to say, Mother?"

All heads turned toward the woman who'd remained rooted to the spot by the wagon during the exchange. She was a beautiful woman, but the color in her face was completely gone. She looked stunned, and Ben thought she even appeared scared as he walked toward her. He kept his arms in tight fists at his sides to keep himself from grabbing her around the neck and demanding her to tell him what was going on.

She backed away as he approached, and then he felt Everly's hand on his arm, stopping him in his tracks.

"Ben, this is my stepmother, Lucy Elliott."

He noticed the look she gave the woman and knew there was no great love between them. "If she is your stepmother, why isn't her last name Wilder? I would assume she was married to your father?"

Hazel decided to step in again. "That's what I've been

trying to tell you, Ben. Lucy was married to Everly's father – not her mother! Her mother was never married to him. She had three children with a man who was married to another woman, after he met her working in a brothel! Is that the kind of family history you want tarnishing your own niece's reputations?"

Hazel was positively screaming at this point with the knowledge that she now had something that would give her some leverage. She was going to win, and even Ben wouldn't be able to fight against what he was obviously finding out for the first time. He had to think of his nieces above all else and marrying a woman with a past like that would not be acceptable in society, even he had to realize that.

Ben turned to Hazel with a look on his face that caused her certainty to waver just a bit. She backed up a few steps, so Ben walked closer to her. He spoke in a very quiet voice, so calm that no one would've believed the fury he was feeling. "I've had just about all I am going to take from you, you spiteful woman. If you keep spouting lies to try and get me to change my mind so I'll marry your daughter, you'll have a long wait. I would rather cut off my own arms with a blunt knife than ever be related to you in any way. Do I make myself clear?" By now he was directly in Hazel's face, and he could see the pulse in her temple.

The door to the porch slammed shut, breaking the showdown between Ben and Hazel.

"All right, everyone needs to just back up and calm down so we can get this sorted," Jake said. "I want to know if I've been duped into becoming partners with someone who has ill intentions towards my cousin's future wife," Jake looked directly at Andrew while he spoke, then turned his attention toward Lucy.

"And if I have, you both better get on your horses and get as far away from me as you can, before I have a chance to get on my horse to follow you." He made it clear that he was not going to be messed with.

Ben looked at Everly and noticed that she wouldn't look him in the eye. She was looking down at the ground. He wanted to rush over and wrap her in his arms, telling her everything would be all right. She looked broken, and he wasn't sure what he could do to fix it. In that moment, he was sure he was about to lose everything.

CHAPTER 15

Everly stood back while Ben demanded Hazel get off his property. She wasn't prepared to back down, but when he quietly strode toward her with barely contained fury, she'd been smart enough to understand the dangerous situation she was in. She'd quickly got back in the wagon with the other women she had brought from town, assuring him she would be back for the children as she drove away.

Everly looked at her stepmother. She'd seen her a few times around the city with her father, when she was still too young to realize she wasn't supposed to approach her father when he was with his real family. She remembered the time she had first seen him with her, and not knowing the situation, had ran over to hug him. Her mother had quickly grabbed her and pulled her away. She'd been so confused about why her mother hadn't even said hello to her father. She also remembered the look on the other woman's face, and she knew she'd done something wrong.

Now, her stepmother had a look on her face that

Everly recognized as a combination of shock and sorrow. She was sure it was very much like the one she had on her own face those many years ago.

Lucy looked toward her, and softly spoke, "I'm sorry, Everly. I never knew that woman would be so spiteful! I never meant for things to get so heated. I wanted to make you pay, for something that wasn't even your fault. My bitterness got the best of me, and I'm so sorry. I never thought she would threaten to take those girls away!"

Everly almost felt sorry for her. She could see that Lucy truly hadn't thought things through, and never had planned for any of this. She'd wanted to stop her from marrying so they wouldn't get the money. But things had taken a horrible turn. Now Ben faced the possibility of losing his nieces, and those girls risked losing the last bit of family they had.

She also knew that all the blame wasn't on Lucy. If she'd told Ben the truth about her background from the very beginning, he wouldn't have ever sent for her and she wouldn't have even had the chance to come out here. Now, she'd fallen in love with the man who would surely hate her, not to mention how much she'd come to care for the girls he had needed her to look after. And now he might lose everything because she hadn't told him the truth.

Never in her life had she felt such sadness for what she was about to lose.

Ben still stood in the middle of the yard looking like he'd been punched in the stomach, and she could tell he didn't know what to do first. So many unanswered questions, and everyone else just stood watching Hazel's wagon become a cloud of dust in the distance.

"Mother, did you set all of this up? Did you arrange

for me to meet up with the Montgomerys, knowing Everly was here? How did you even know?"

Everly's stepbrother, or whatever he would be to her since he was no blood relation at all, was the first to break the silence. Ben was still just standing there looking at the wagon retreating down the road. She knew he was desperately trying to figure out how he could fix this situation.

"I'm sorry, Andrew. I saw a paper in the lawyer's office with Ben Montgomery's name on it and where he lived. It had Everly's name on it too, and I knew something was up. I'd been in the store when they picked up the magazine looking for brides out west, and I put everything together. When I found out that Ben and his family were looking for a partner out east for working with their horses, I knew this was the perfect chance for you. You've worked so hard to build your own horse-breeding business, and this was a huge opportunity for you. The fact that I might be able to stop Everly from following through with the terms of Thomas' will was an added bonus, one that I now regret terribly." She choked on the last words as she looked once again towards Everly.

"When we got to town, I overheard Hazel talking to a woman in the store about Ben having a woman out here he was planning to marry. I could tell she wasn't happy with the arrangement either, so I approached her and mentioned that if she did some digging, she might find out some more about Everly's past that could help her stop it. I gave her some details, but I swear I didn't tell her everything. She must have done some investigating on her own."

With the last words, she started to cry. "I was just always so angry and hurt that I couldn't give Thomas any children of our own. Knowing he had a whole other family the entire time he was married to me broke my heart. I tried so hard to make him happy, but he could never give me the love I knew he had for Caroline. It wasn't Everly's fault, but in my grief and anger, I couldn't see that."

Lucy turned to Jake. "Please don't punish my son for my mistakes. I truly do believe he is the best man for this job. He had no idea of any of this."

Ben walked over to Lucy. "I still don't know exactly what has happened here, but I would suggest that you all leave until I have a chance to figure out what I'm going to do."

He turned to his father. "Take them all back to your place and I'll be around later so we can discuss things. I need to deal with my family first."

With that, he turned and walked into the house, leaving them all there to watch his retreating back. Lucy looked toward Everly again with tears in her eyes. "I'm so sorry, Everly." She turned and climbed back into the wagon. Ben's father took up the reins, and Andrew mounted his horse while shooting Everly an apologetic look. They all rode out of the yard leaving only Sarah and Jake standing there with her. As Everly looked at Jake, she sensed that he was barely controlling his anger.

"Everly, you'd better start explaining things to Ben so he can figure out how to fix this. Why didn't you just tell him from the beginning? He would've understood. At least he would have been able to prepare, but now he's been blindsided. You do realize he could lose his nieces because of this?" Jake was shaking he was so angry, and Everly didn't blame him.

Before she could say anything though, Sarah walked over to Jake and put her face directly in front of his, while poking his chest with her finger. "How dare you question anything that Everly has done? She did all of this for us. She agreed to get married to a complete stranger, move out west, away from the only home she has known, all for us. For her sisters and her mother who were going to be left with nothing. She didn't ever ask for any of this, and only tried to protect everyone from a past that all of us would rather be left there."

Everly had never seen Sarah so angry, and the look on Jake's face told her he hadn't expected such fury from her either.

Sarah turned and walked over to Everly. "Come on. We don't need to stay here anymore. I won't let them treat you like you've done something wrong."

"No, Sarah. I need to at least try to fix things so Ben won't lose the girls. Wait here for me. We'll leave after I've had a chance to talk to him."

She was scared to leave the two of them alone out here, but she had to speak to Ben. After seeing Sarah a minute ago, she had no doubt she could handle herself with Jake.

She set her bag on the porch and walked in the door. Ben was sitting in his chair with both girls tucked on his lap, crying. The look on their faces, and Ben's, broke her heart. She'd come out here thinking only of herself, and her own situation, not realizing that her past could cause so much trouble for Ben. She should have thought through what could happen to this family. She should have let him find someone more suitable. Someone who would have been good for the girls, and who Hazel would have no dirt on to take them away.

"I just want to say how sorry I am. I should've told you the truth about my past. Unfortunately, when I came out here, I was only thinking of my problems and now I've hurt all of you. I never meant for this to happen."

She stood with her hands folded in front of her, while she looked at this family she'd come to love.

"You should have just been honest with me, Everly. You never even gave me the chance to decide. You didn't trust me enough to let me know. I wouldn't have cared. But at least I could have prepared myself for the chance that Hazel would use this against me." He ran his fingers through his hair again, something she noticed he did when he was angry.

By now, the girls were watching them both with big eyes. "Please don't fight. We don't want you to fight. Don't be mad at her, Uncle Ben. Everly is nice and she wouldn't do anything mean." Olivia looked at Everly and smiled at her.

"Girls, you go on and play." Ben stood up and shooed the girls off the porch. They looked back at Everly with worry, knowing that she was in trouble. She gave them a reassuring smile and told them she would be fine.

Left alone with Ben, and the way he was looking at her, tore at her heart. She knew she'd hurt him by not letting him know everything. His eyes were a combination of anger and pain, and she desperately wanted to have him look at her like he had this morning before everything had fallen apart.

She took a deep breath as she sat down in a chair beside Ben. She looked down at her folded hands in her lap as she spoke. "My mom was orphaned as a young gir, and had no family to go to. She lived on the streets and was taken in by a woman who put her to work in her brothel. When she got older, she ended up having to..." Her words trailed off as a lump formed in her throat as it always did when she had to talk about what her mother had to endure to survive. She loved her mother and thinking about the life she'd been forced to live saddened her right through to her soul.

She sat up straighter and continued. "My father came into the brothel one night, as I guess men do. He took a liking to my mother, and came back regularly, eventually taking her out of the brothel and setting her up in an apartment above a hotel. He owned the hotel. He was a very wealthy man, although none of us ever got to see any finery because of it." She had a bitterness in her voice as she always felt when she spoke about her father.

She stood up and looked out across the yard. She could see Sarah comforting the girls, sitting on the ground with them and hugging them. Those poor girls looked terrified. They were old enough to understand something terrible had just happened. After everything they'd already been through in their lives, Everly felt a weight of responsibility for causing them more pain. As she watched, Jake paced back and forth, said something to Sarah, then hopped on his horse and tore off down the road leaving nothing but a cloud of dust behind.

She turned back to Ben.

"My mother was a kept woman. But my father never gave her more than enough to just get by. I hated him. Not always though. When I was a little girl, I remember him coming to the apartment and he would sometimes talk to me. Most of the time, though, we girls were just a nuisance to him. I overheard him one time talking with Mama. He said if just one of the women in his life could have given him a son, he could have been happy. I know Mama cried so hard that night, and after that I hated him for what he was doing to her."

As she remembered that time, she finally felt the tears start to flow down her cheeks.

"It's all right, Everly. I know. You don't need to

explain anymore," Ben reassured her. The fact that he was trying to comfort her, after all the pain she'd caused him today, made her feel worse.

"No, Ben. You have to let me finish. It's the least I can do before I leave. You deserve to know the truth."

He stood up and walked over to where she was standing. "You aren't going anywhere, Everly."

"Yes, I am. With me gone, you can marry someone suitable and Hazel will back off. Once she has no more reason for taking the girls from you, you can go back to living your life in peace. I'd hoped my past wouldn't make a difference, but with a woman like Hazel determined to win, it was the worst thing I could have brought out here for you to deal with.

"I have my things packed, and I just want to say goodbye to the girls. You'll never know how much I've truly enjoyed being here with all of you..." Another lump formed in her throat, cutting off her words as she turned to go.

Ben reached out and grabbed her arm. "I said you aren't going anywhere, Everly. And I meant it."

She tried to pull her arm free. She had to get away from him because she knew as long as she was this close to him, she wouldn't be able to think clearly.

He pulled her in more and put his arms around her. "Everly, don't you know by now that I won't ever let you go? I couldn't even if I wanted to," he sighed the words, as he rested his forehead on hers.

The tears kept flowing as she looked up at his face. The face she'd come to love, which broke her heart as she realized just how much she had to lose now.

His eyes looked into hers. "I don't care about your mother's past. I hate what your father did to you all of those years, but I can't say I hate him for it, because without those terms in his will, you'd never be here."

She wasn't sure she was hearing him right. He should be so angry with her, but the way he was looking at her didn't show any anger at all.

"But I've caused so much trouble today," Everly said. "If I'd been honest in the beginning you wouldn't have even sent money to bring me out here. Everyone would have been better off."

He raised his hand and cupped her cheek. His fingers wiped away her tears as they ran down her face.

"I don't know what I would've done if you'd been honest with me, but the fact is you're here now and I know I would never be better off without you. You've managed to become a part of my life so completely since the moment you stepped off the train, there is no way I could now, or ever, let you go."

With that, he lowered his head and pressed his lips to hers. She kissed him back with an urgency she'd never known before. All she knew was that this feeling, right now, was all she needed. Nothing else mattered.

He raised his head and looked down at her. "I love you, Everly Wilder, and nothing – no vindictive women, no tainted past – will make me ever change my mind."

She started to cry again, but this time, they were tears of such joy she felt she would burst. Ben's face dropped as he watched her, not expecting tears after professing his love.

She smiled and lifted her hands to his cheeks. "I love you too, Ben. You've given me more happiness in this short time with you than I've ever known in my whole life. I never thought I could give myself to a man, thinking they would only hurt me, but you've shown me that some men can be honorable."

She pulled his head back down to hers, kissing him with a passion that had them both gasping for air. Ben groaned as he lifted his head. "We have to stop this now, or I'm not so sure how honorable I can continue to be."

Everly felt her cheeks heat up as she realized how wanton she'd been. He caressed her cheek again, while smiling at her with a love she could feel right through to her heart.

The moment was broken by steps on the porch, and the sound of Sarah clearing her throat.

Everly pulled away from Ben and put her arms out to the girls who were standing watching them both intently. They ran to her, burying their faces in her neck.

"Well, I guess now we should figure out what to do next before Hazel gets back." Everly cringed as the mood was broken by Ben's words.

She smiled down at the girls, assuring them that everything would be all right, even if she didn't feel that sure herself.

"That's what I thought I should come in and tell you. Jake left here a few minutes ago muttering to himself about you having kept quiet long enough. Something about why you didn't marry that horrible woman's daughter, and then he said a few words I can't repeat about not caring anymore about anyone else's reputation. Then he hopped on his horse and yelled back to tell you he'd take care of that meddling old goat once and for all," Sarah filled them in.

Ben cursed as he took off toward the barn.

Everly ran after him. "What are you doing? Where are you going?"

"Just stay here with the girls. I'll be right back, and hopefully all of this will be behind us once and for all," he shouted as he ran for his horse.

CHAPTER 16

Everly paced the floor, wringing her hands while the others sat eating some lunch that Sarah had made. The morning had been such a blur, it was hard to believe that just a few hours ago, she'd been sitting in this kitchen telling everyone she'd agreed to become Ben's wife. If she had only known what was to come.

Ben had told her he loved her. Those were words she never believed she'd hear from a man, and she honestly hadn't known how badly she wanted to hear them. Hearing them come from Ben's lips filled her with such joy and knowing that he wasn't going to just walk away from her after everything that had happened this morning gave her hope.

When she heard the pounding of hooves coming into the yard, she ran out the door before the others even had a chance to hear them.

She saw Ben and Jake riding their horses. Behind them was Andrew on his horse, Ben's father with Lucy in the wagon, and another wagon that looked like Mary and her family. There was another man on a horse that she thought looked familiar, but she couldn't place him.

She stood there unsure what to do. She didn't know what Ben and Jake had been up to when they went into town, and she was nervous to find out. Even though Ben had told her she wasn't going anywhere, if it came down to him losing the girls because of her, she didn't care what he said. She wouldn't be staying if that were to happen.

Ben dismounted from his horse, and walked toward her while the rest pulled into the yard. He kept coming closer, never taking his eyes off her. She swallowed hard, unsure if she should go to him or if he was angry.

When he got to the porch, he put his hand out to her. She put her hand in his, and he smiled. What was going on?

"Everly, I think it's time we got married before someone else tries to stop us." He was looking at her with such intensity she wasn't sure how she was supposed to answer.

"But what about Hazel and everything else that's happened and..." her words trailed off as he shook his head.

"It doesn't matter. Hazel won't bother us anymore, and I don't care about anything else. This morning you said you would marry me, and I'm holding you to that right now."

Her eyes widened as it sank in that Hazel wouldn't bother them anymore. "What did you do to Hazel?" she gasped, afraid to hear the answer as she turned her eyes toward Jake.

Jake chuckled at Everly's reaction as he had stood quietly to the side. "We didn't hurt her or do anything drastic like that," he laughed. "Although if I had my way it might have been different," he muttered that last bit under his breath as he turned back to the horses and led them to the barn.

Ben filled her in, "We just mentioned something to her that would possibly ruin her own daughter's reputation. I'd never told her, but when I was courting her daughter Margaret, Jake caught her with the blacksmith's son. They were only kissing, but it was enough to make me realize I didn't want to be stuck married to someone who was in love with someone else. She'd only ever agreed to marry me because her mother had forced her to. I never told Hazel and had taken the blame for the broken engagement. She's been determined to get me back in her daughter's life ever since. She thought that by threatening to take the girls from me, she had the perfect opportunity to force me to marry — and since there are not many women around here to court, she thought she had me."

"And then you showed up." He took her hands in his. "So, are we getting married or not?"

"Well, what, you mean right now?" Everly sputtered.

"Yes, we have everyone we need right here. The minister has come with me from town, and I stopped along the way and invited some guests. I'm not taking any more chances that you'll try to get away from me, Everly Wilder."

Everly looked around at everyone who was standing around her. Even her stepmother was smiling at her. She was sure she was dreaming and had to look back toward Ben to make sure he was really there.

He led her down off the porch, and over to the minister who had accompanied them from town. As they stood in front of him, Ben took her hand and tucked it in tightly under his arm.

He leaned down and whispered, "No one will ever take the people I love from me. And that includes you, Everly." With that, he bent down and kissed her so tenderly, she felt her knees grow weak. He steadied her with his hand around her waist.

She knew she had found home.

EPILOGUE

Everly sat watching the festivities around her. The past week had been a blur. They'd got married the very afternoon Ben had come back from town, with just their few friends and family around them.

Ben wanted her to have more though, so he'd sent for her mom, her youngest sister Bethany and even Mr. McConnell. They'd all arrived within just a few days, and they had thrown a party to celebrate the marriage of Ben and Everly. It seemed like the entire community of High Ridge had shown up, except for Hazel Hayes, and everyone was thrilled to welcome her into their lives.

She'd never known her heart to feel so full. She watched as her mom danced with Mr. McConnell and noticed them looking at each other with happy smiles. She turned her head slightly as she noticed Lucy dance past with Ben's father and thought how nice it was to see both women enjoying themselves with men who were treating them so well.

Ben was standing to the side talking with Jake,

Andrew and some men from town. After the dust had all settled, they'd realized that Andrew knew nothing about the situation and had never intended any harm to Everly. He was still considered to be the best for the job and was fitting in very well with the men. She was glad because she knew his childhood likely didn't have very many happy memories either.

Alistair McConnell walked over and sat down beside her after the town minister asked Caroline to dance. She couldn't help but notice how young and happy her mom seemed, more than she ever remembered her being in her whole life.

"I love seeing that smile on your face, Everly." Alistair smiled as he looked at her. "You're obviously happy with your decision to move out here and get married."

"I must confess I've never felt happiness like this before. Ben and the girls have given me something I didn't even know I was looking for." She looked out at the people around them, then laughed. "It's funny how things turn out. If it weren't for my father, I wouldn't have ever followed this path. I would never have known what I was missing. So, as much as I am angry with my father, I have to feel some gratitude towards him too."

He reached over and took her hand. "Your father wasn't a perfect man, and he knew that. He struggled with the feelings he had for both your mother and then Lucy after they were married. He desperately wanted a son, and he regretted making you girls feel like you didn't measure up. He did love you all, even if he didn't know how to show it."

Everly couldn't look at him for fear she would choke up. Talking about her father was difficult for her and hearing that he did care for her was sometimes hard to believe.

"He knew you would never trust a man after growing up with him in and out of your life like he was. He wanted more for you, which is why he put those demands in his will. He knew he had to do something to keep you from spending your whole life hating men and never finding your own happiness."

She was torn between the feelings of hate she'd always had for the man, and new feelings she couldn't understand. Knowing he'd cared about her and her sisters wasn't something she was used to. But she had to agree that she would never have let a man get close to her if not for what he had done.

Alistair continued as he stood up to go back out and claim his spot with Caroline on the makeshift dance floor. "Hopefully someday you'll be able to forgive your father just a bit for bad decisions he might have made. He was human, and he made mistakes he regretted. He would be very proud of you today. I know I am. And I'm glad to be able to be here to celebrate with you."

"Thank you, Mr. McConnell. You've always been there for us, and I'm so glad you're here too." She nudged her head towards the dance floor. "Now, you better get back out there before someone else cuts in."

He pulled her close for a hug, then turned and walked back over where Caroline was talking with some of the women from town.

Ben caught her eye from across the wooden floor they'd put together to dance on in their front yard. He winked at her, and she felt warm inside as she could see the longing in his eyes even from that distance. He started to push away from the tree he'd been leaning on while talking with the men but stopped as he noticed her sisters rush over to her. He smiled and shrugged, knowing he'd have to wait his turn.

"Everly! Why aren't you up dancing?" Sarah had been dancing all evening and was out of breath as she sat down in a chair beside her.

"I'm just taking a rest. The past few days have been a bit of a whirlwind, and I was just taking a moment to enjoy watching everyone I care about together and having fun." Everly realized just how much those words meant, as she looked around and watched the people before her laughing and enjoying the festivities.

"This dress is itching me, but I'll admit I'm even having a bit of fun too." Beth had danced a few times, taking turns with Ben, Jake and Alistair. She had a smile on her face that gave away her youthful innocence, and Everly was so happy to see her feeling this way. She couldn't remember ever seeing Beth so relaxed and happy.

"Mama and Mr. McConnell have sure been dancing a lot together. Have you guys noticed how they're looking at each other?" Sarah had noticed, and Beth nodded her head in agreement.

The girls sat quietly for a few moments watching the dancers, and just enjoyed being together again. They were all happy to be together, and no one seemed willing to break the moment.

"Thank you, Everly," Beth was the first to break the silence.

Startled, Everly turned and looked at Beth. "For what?"

"For everything. For always taking care of us. For always putting us first. You came out here willing to get married, even though you knew nothing about what you were coming out here for. You did it all for us, and you didn't need to. But you did." Everly felt both her hands being taken by her sisters, and she could feel tears welling up in her eyes.

"We are so glad everything worked out so well for you. You deserve to be happy," Sarah added.

Everly looked at the young ladies in front of her, and felt a sadness knowing they'd be leaving tomorrow to go back home. They'd always been together, and even though she was happy to be here with Ben, she was still going to miss these girls she'd spent her years growing up with.

Trying to get her mind on other things, she decided to ask Sarah about what had gone on between her and Jake. They seemed to be at odds with each other a great deal, and she couldn't understand what had happened to cause the friction.

When she posed the question, Sarah looked across the crowd of people toward where Jake stood talking with Andrew. Ben had taken Caroline onto the dance floor, and they were laughing together as they bumped into other couples wrestling for room on the small wooden planks.

She didn't say anything for a minute, and Everly thought maybe she wasn't going to tell them anything.

"I don't know how to explain it. He seemed so nice when we met, and I thought maybe I sensed something between us. But as we spent more time together, it was as if he didn't want to be anywhere near me."

Everly watched as Sarah kept her eyes on Jake as she spoke. She noticed the moment when Jake looked over to where they were sitting and saw his eyes fall on Sarah. When their eyes met, Sarah turned her head away, but Jake never took his eyes off her.

Now that she'd gone through what seemed like so much

with Ben to get to the point they were at, she felt she was able to understand the confusion he was likely going through with his feelings towards her sister. Ben had told her how Jake had been hurt by a woman in the past, and now had a difficult time trusting them. She could relate to that.

She reached her hand over and took Sarah's in her own. "I'm sure it isn't you he is running from, but his own feelings and mistrust. Give him some time and see where things go."

"I don't have the time, Everly. I'm heading home with Mama, Beth and Mr. McConnell tomorrow." Everly could feel Sarah's heartbreak and wished she knew how to fix it.

Just then a slower song came on, and Ben walked toward her, putting his hand out to pull her up to dance with him. "Well, Mrs. Montgomery, I feel like I haven't seen you all evening, so would you be able to give me this dance?" His eyes sparkled as he spoke to her, and she couldn't wait to feel his arms around her while they danced.

She looked at her sisters to make sure Sarah was all right, and they nodded to the dance floor with happy smiles on their faces. "Get going and spend some time with your husband!" As Sarah spoke, Jake walked over and put his hand out. Without saying a word, she took his hand and they walked to the dance floor.

Ben raised an eyebrow as he watched Jake's retreating back but didn't say anything. Beth wasn't left sitting alone as Andrew came over and bowed to her for a dance. He'd spent the past few days getting to know all of them, and Everly was sure he'd never had any ill feelings towards them. He had been hurt just as much as the rest of them had been by her father.

As Ben's arms went around her, Everly felt her head

bow down onto his shoulder. She felt so content and happy in his arms.

"Well, Everly Montgomery, I finally get a moment alone with my wife. Have you had fun today with all of the festivities, family and friends?"

She looked up into his eyes and smiled. "Everything has been perfect. I've never felt so happy. But, I can't wait to be alone with you again."

His eyes darkened as he looked down at her. "Your wish is my command." With those words, he lifted her into his arms, and carried her toward the house. The crowd around them cheered as she buried her face in his chest. "Ben! What will everyone think?"

"I imagine they'll be thinking there is a man who loves his wife, who is happier than he's ever been in his life, and who can't wait another minute to be alone with the woman he will spend the rest of his days with."

As their lips met, Everly could feel the love between them and she knew she would never be happier than she was at this moment.

ABOUT THE AUTHOR

USA Today Bestselling Author Kay P. Dawson writes sweet western romance – the kind that leaves out all of the juicy details and immerses you in a true, heartfelt love story. Growing up pretending she was Laura Ingalls, she's always had a love for the old west and pioneer times. She believes in true love, and finding your happy ever after.

Happily married mom of two girls, Kay has always taught her children to follow their dreams. And, after a breast cancer diagnosis at the age of 39, she realized it was time to take her own advice. She had always wanted to write a book, and she decided that the someday she was waiting for was now.

She writes western historical, contemporary and time travel romance that all transport the reader to a time or place where true love always finds a way.